Pure
Luck

Pure Luck

- A Novel -

KATHRYN B. HULL

Copyright © 2024 by Kathryn B. Hull

All rights reserved. No part of this publication may be reproduced, distributed, or transmitted in any form or by any means, including photocopying, recording, or other electronic or mechanical methods, without the prior written permission of the copyright owner and the publisher, except in the case of brief quotations embodied in critical reviews and certain other noncommercial uses permitted by copyright law. For permission requests, write to the publisher, addressed "Attention: Permissions Coordinator," at the address below.

ARPress
45 Dan Road Suite 5
Canton MA 02021

Hotline: 1(888) 821-0229
Fax: 1(508) 545-7580

Ordering Information:

Quantity sales. Special discounts are available on quantity purchases by corporations, associations, and others. For details, contact the publisher at the address above.

Printed in the United States of America.

ISBN-13:   Softcover   979-8-89356-216-3
                eBook   979-8-89356-217-0

Library of Congress Control Number: 2024908176

This book is dedicated to children everywhere, including my children, Laurice, Craig, and Eric.

CONTENTS

ACKNOWLEDGMENTS

Thanks to Alan Boehmer, a delightful host whose home on the central coast of California was where I began the story. It provided the inspiration and setting for the children's adventure. And to the editor par excellence, Alice Bailes Bell, who gave great encouragement and direction.

A BIRTHDAY DISCOVERY

Jennifer had no way of knowing this would be her lucky day. That's the way it is with luck—you never know when it will strike. Randy had said there was no such thing as luck, that you make your own. But sometimes things just happen to you. That has to be luck, good or bad. That's the way it was last Sunday—pure luck.

Jennifer and Randy had been best friends since they were five years old when his family moved next door to her. Their birthdays were only nine days apart, and so they always celebrated them together. This year was no different. On a special Saturday in June, they invited twelve of their best friends, one for each of their years, to come to their party. There was music and dancing, snacks, birthday cake with ice cream, and more than enough gifts for any twelve-year-old.

"That was the best party ever!" Jennifer said to Randy after all their friends had left.

"Yeah, it was," Randy agreed. "And we got some great stuff."

"But the present from our parents is the best one. I can hardly wait to go to the beach and try it out."

"Let's go first thing in the morning," Randy said. "We can take a lunch and spend the day there looking for treasures in the sand."

"Good idea. I'll make some sandwiches. You bring the sodas and something for snacks. Okay?"

"Sure. See ya tomorrow then," Randy said as he gathered up his gifts. "I wonder what we will find."

"Who knows? Just be ready around nine!" Jennifer shouted after him as he walked out of the kitchen and went to his house next door. She picked up her presents and took them to her room. She caught a glimpse of herself in the mirror and stopped. She saw a slender, dark-haired girl with deep brown eyes looking back at her.

"Yes, it's been a good birthday," she said to the image. "And the last one before becoming a teenager. I wonder if it will feel different to be thirteen." She stood there looking at her reflection for several minutes wondering how another year might bring changes and what they would be. *Whatever happens,* she thought, *I know Randy will always be my best friend.*

By nine the next morning, Randy appeared at the back door with a red and white cooler in hand. He was dressed in cut-off jeans with a red tee shirt. A red and white baseball cap covered his blond hair. "Hey, Jen!" he shouted as he opened the door and walked in. "Come on. Let's go!"

"Be right there," she answered from her room. She came bounding into the kitchen, sneakers in hand, her hair pulled back into a neat ponytail, and wearing red shorts with a red and white striped tee shirt. Sandwiches sat on the cutting board waiting to be put in the cooler. She slipped on her shoes and bounced up from the chair. "I hope I made enough sandwiches," she said as she put them in the cooler. "Here, you carry this, and I'll get the thing from our parents. What's it called?"

"A metal detector."

"Oh, right." She picked it up from the back porch and looped the headphones around her neck. "Mom, we're on our way. See ya later!" she shouted as they ran down the steps and set off for the day's adventure. The short walk to the beach was filled with excited chatter.

"What do you suppose we'll find?" Jennifer asked.

"Oh, probably some bottle caps, maybe some money, and who knows what else."

"It'd be great if we found a lot of money."

"Yeah. But we'll be lucky if we find any."

"Whatever we find, we share fifty-fifty—if it's worth anything, of course," Jennifer said.

"Naturally. The detector was given to both of us, so whatever it finds belongs to both of us—equally."

They walked into the cove sheltered by sand dunes and a rocky cliff. "We need to find a place to put the cooler," Randy said.

"How about over there under that rocky ledge? It's out of the sun," Jennifer said as she pointed to the steep cliff at the end of the sandy beach.

"Yeah, that looks like a good spot."

They tucked it as far out of sight as they could and took off to explore the sand for treasures. Randy held the detector in front of him as they walked back and forth, making a crisscross pattern in the sand. Nothing was registering on the meter, and the soft static-like sound coming through the headphones never changed. Nearly half an hour had gone by, and there was nothing for their effort.

"Maybe this thing doesn't work," Jennifer said, a frown creasing her forehead.

"Well, let's test it." Randy held it over his watch. The meter jumped. "See. It works."

"Okay then, let's keep going."

In a few minutes, Randy saw a slight movement of the needle but no change in the sound. "Wait. It moved." He stopped over the spot in the sand where the needle had moved. "Here!"

Jennifer began to dig into the sand. About six or eight inches down, her fingers touched something hard. "There's something here!" A little more digging and she pulled out a shell. "Well, that can't be what the detector found. It's not metal. But it is beautiful. I think I'll keep it," she said as she brushed off the sand and put it in her pocket.

Randy put the detector over the hole in the sand, and the meter registered a stronger signal. "There's still something there. Keep digging."

"We should have brought a shovel. This is hard to do with just my hands. Here, you dig for a while."

Randy handed the detector and earphones to Jennifer, and getting down on his knees, he began digging with both hands. The sand kept falling in as the hole got deeper. "Swing it over here, Jen, and see where the signal is the strongest."

Jennifer slowly moved the round disc over the hole, watching the movement of the needle and listening to the static. "Right here," she said, holding it over the side of the hole, which was now nearly a foot deep.

Randy hurriedly began digging in that area, flipping sand out in all directions. The sand was damp this far down, which made the digging harder. His nails were encrusted with it, and it was beginning to feel like sandpaper on the ends of his fingers.

"Hey, I touched something, but it doesn't feel like metal." He continued digging around it and finally saw something about the size of a wallet. He lifted it out. It was a leather pouch, soft from the damp sand and about ready to fall apart. He handed it carefully to Jennifer.

"It's heavy," she said. "There's something in it."

They sat down, their feet in the freshly dug hole, and looked at each other, hesitating just a few seconds before Jennifer began carefully pulling apart the layers of leather. Randy leaned over to see what was inside.

"It *is* money!" he said in surprise. "How much?"

Jennifer took the coins out one at a time and placed them in Randy's outstretched hand.

"These don't look like any coins I've ever seen," Randy said. "They're a different size from ours. They're so discolored, probably from being buried a long time, that it's hard to tell what they are."

"Maybe it's pirates' treasure that's been buried here for a hundred years or longer," Jennifer suggested with a hint of mystery in her voice. "If it is, we might find more."

"Oh, sure. As if there were such a thing as pirates in this area."

"Well, we don't know how long this has been buried here, so maybe there used to be pirates around—a long time ago."

Randy held a dozen or more salt-encrusted coins in his hands. When Jennifer peeled the last one off the leather, she tossed the pouch aside and leaned over to study the coins. A loose strand of hair fell across her face. She pulled it back and tucked it behind her ear.

"Let's look for some more," she said to Randy as she pulled her feet out of the hole, stood up, and picked up the detector. "If it was left here by pirates, maybe they dropped it on the way to bury a much bigger treasure," she said hopefully.

"Hey, even if that's not true, it would be fun to pretend. So where would they hide treasure?" Randy asked as he looked up the beach toward the rocks. "Maybe there's a cave in there, one that you find only when the tide's out."

"It's out now, so let's go see."

FOLLOWİNG A STRAİGHT LİNE

Randy led the way, and Jennifer held the metal detector close to the sand as she slowly followed him. "Hey, I think there's something here." She stopped and held the detector over a spot in the sand where the needle moved. Randy began digging.

"It's just a rusty piece of metal," Randy said with disappointment. "It looks a little bit like a nail, but it's square. Where do you think it's from?"

"The pirates' ship, of course," Jennifer said with a teasing smile.

"In that case, I'll keep it," he said with a grin. He put it in his pocket.

They continued in a straight line toward the rocks with Jennifer listening to the static in the earphones and watching for any movement of the meter. They were in such quiet concentration that Jennifer jumped in surprise when the detector suddenly registered a find. She dropped it on the sand and began digging. In a little while, she lifted out a small round disc.

"It's hard to tell what this is, but maybe we've found another coin," she said. "It looks worse than the others, probably because it wasn't protected from the salt and sand like those we found in the leather pouch."

Randy dropped the coin in his pocket with the others and said, "Now if we find even one more, it may lead us in the direction of the big treasure."

They walked several steps farther toward the cliff and soon heard another positive signal on the detector. Randy was digging immediately, and under about eight inches of sand he found a disc very much like the last one.

"Now, if we make a straight line through the places where we found these, it should point us to the hidden treasure." He squatted in the sand and drew an imaginary line across the beach. It went to a large outcropping of rocks that caught the splash of a wave every time one rolled in.

"It can't be there. There's no opening," Jennifer said as she squinted toward the cliff.

"Maybe there's a cave or something on the other side. It's too steep to climb. We just have to get around it when the wave goes out."

"But we don't know what's on the other side. What if we get caught by a wave?" Jennifer said with concern.

"I'll go first," said Randy. "And then if it's okay, I'll call you, and you can come as the next wave goes out."

"But if you don't find a place to go where you can be safe from the water, what will you do?"

"I'll probably have to swim back," Randy said with a slight look of fear on his freckled face. "But I'm a good swimmer. I'll make it," he said with a little more confidence.

"I don't know," Jennifer said. "We'd better think about this."

"Well, it looks like the tide isn't all the way out yet, so let's get something to eat and watch for the best time to go."

"Good idea. I'm getting hungry anyway." Jennifer turned toward the place where she had left the cooler, and Randy followed, holding the detector over the sand as he walked. He found nothing more.

They sat leaning against the cliff and facing the waves so they could tell when the tide was lower and it would be safe to go around the rocky cliff. Seagulls were searching for their midday feast, diving into the water while the sand-colored godwits walked along the shoreline dipping their bills into the royal blue water, eating their way down the beach. An occasional white egret walked chest deep in the gently receding waves, looking for a tasty tidbit, squawking loudly at any approaching creature. It fluttered across the surface of the water chasing small fish and then diving down to catch one. It was fun watching the birds have their lunch while they ate theirs.

Jennifer had made Randy's favorite: peanut butter and jelly sandwiches. That's what he'd had every day for lunch since he started school, and he never traded for anything. They each took a soda and sat quietly watching the activity on the water and thinking about the hidden treasure.

"What do you think we'll find if there is a cave around there?" Jennifer wondered out loud.

"A pirates' chest full of gold, of course," Randy said with a laugh.

"It could be possible, you know. Maybe no one's ever been around that cliff to see what's on the other side."

"We're explorers. We'll be the first."

"Well, if we're going to go, we'd better get moving. I think the tide is at its lowest now. Remember, if we do make it, we still have to get back. We can't be there very long," Jennifer said. She was still a little unsure of the plan.

"We won't need to be there long. We'll just see if there's a place to hide treasure. Then if there is a pirates' chest, we'll come back another time with someone to help us carry it. No problem," he said with a grin, sounding surer of himself than he felt.

"Are you scared?" she asked him.

Randy just shrugged his shoulders.

FİNDİNG A CAVE

They stood at the water's edge watching the waves to see how much time was between them. "There's nothing to this," Randy said. "I'm a good swimmer, if it comes to that." He planned his move to go right after the next big wave. Usually after a big one they were a bit smaller until another big one, maybe seven waves later.

"Listen for me to call and then you run around as fast as you can. And don't drop the detector. We might need it."

"Do you want to take it with you?"

"No, 'cause I might have to swim back. If I can stay there, then it'll be okay for you to come with it."

"Randy, can I come with you?" Jennifer asked. "I don't want to be alone." She was biting her lower lip, which Randy knew meant she was afraid.

"You'll be okay. Just listen for me to call. See you soon, Jen," he said as he raced around the rocky cliff after the big wave crashed against it. He followed it as it retreated down the sandy beach.

Jennifer held her breath, listening for Randy. She counted the roaring waves going in and out—*five, six, seven. That is the big one. Why hasn't Randy called? The crashing waves are so noisy. Maybe I can't hear him.* She looked into the waves expecting to see him swimming, but there was no sign of him. If she was going to get around the rocks, and if they could find the treasure and then get back before the tide came in, he'd better call her pretty soon. *Maybe I should just go ahead on my own,* she thought. *Maybe he's hurt or something. How long should I wait? This was a crazy idea.* She walked down as close to the cliff as she could, waiting for the right time to run around it. *The next wave should be the one,* she said to herself. Just as she was poised, detector in hand, she heard a faint voice call her name. The wave crashed. Her heart was pounding as she ran, following it on its way back toward the ocean.

Around the point of rocks, she saw a narrow strip of sand next to the steep cliff but no Randy. She ran toward the cliff as the next wave covered her feet. "Randy! Where are you?" she shouted.

"Around here. Just run fast."

She heard his voice from around the next large rock. Her shoes squished as she ran through the retreating wave, turning the corner just as the next one came crashing on the rocks. She was getting wet, but so far she wasn't going to have to swim. She held the detector above her head to keep it dry and called, "Randy, where do I go?"

Randy answered, "Just around one more rock. Run, Jen! Now!"

Jennifer followed the wave and ran around the rock to see Randy standing in front of a small opening in the side of the cliff. Jen let out her breath and gasped for air. "Oh, Randy, I'm glad you're okay."

"Over here," he called. "I think I've found it."

"Found what?" she yelled as she ran toward him.

"A place where a treasure chest could be. Come on. Let's explore it." Randy sounded excited. He went a few steps up the side of the bank and reached his hand down to help Jennifer climb up. He led the way into an opening just wide enough for them to squeeze in. "It's too dark to see very much. I wish we had a flashlight," Randy said as he bumped his head on the top of the cave. "Just keep your head down and move over a little bit so the light can come in."

"This opening is so small, no grown-up could ever get in here to bury a treasure."

"Well, just maybe it was a small pirate who did it. Let's wait a minute for our eyes to get used to the dark. We can feel around for a spot that's different."

"Good thinking," Jennifer said as she moved her hand over the floor of the cave. The surface was damp, and she could feel the smoothness of the dirt as if it had been packed down. "Oh, this is way too hard to dig with just our hands. We have to get a shovel or something."

"We could come back tomorrow with a shovel and a light."

"Let's not chance it," Randy said as he turned to go out of the cave. We have to be sure we get back around the rocks before the tide comes in. I'd love to know if there really is a treasure buried here, but I sure don't want to be caught by the tide and have to spend the night in this place."

"You're right. We'd better go while we still can get around the rocks. What if the tide gets high enough that it even comes in here?"

"Maybe this was the den for some animals or even sea lions," she said. "I just hope there aren't any in here now," she said with a shudder.

"How far back do you think this goes? Maybe something's living in here now, but we can't see it without a light."

"Well, I sure don't want to come face-to-face with some creature I can't see."

Randy thought about that for a bit. He looked into the cliff's hollow as far as he could. "Well, it does get smaller as it goes back, so I don't think a pirate would have put a treasure very far back. He couldn't get in there. If there's anything buried in here, it should be about where we're standing."

Jennifer had been feeling the floor of the cave with her hands. "Try the detector right here where the dirt seems a little higher. Let's see what it does."

Randy picked up the detector and held it over the spot Jennifer pointed to. He could hardly see the needle in the dim light, but the static was much louder than when they had found the leather pouch filled with coins. "I think we've found the treasure!" Randy shouted. "Look at this needle! It's going crazy."

"We don't have time to dig now! We have to get out of here while we can still get around the rocks."

ESCAPING THE WAVES

Suddenly a fluttering sound came from the back of the cave. Jennifer screamed and grabbed Randy. "Come on. Let's get out of here fast."

They scrambled out and down onto the sand, their hearts pounding. Jennifer's legs felt weak and trembling, and as always when she was afraid, she was biting her lower lip.

"What do you think that was," Randy said as he turned to look back at the cave. "Let's watch for a while and see if something comes out."

Nothing did, but Jennifer knew they had heard something, and she was not going back in until she knew what it was.

A big wave came splashing up on the rocks, roaring as it rolled in, covering their feet. The tide was rising, and they were going to be caught, not able to get around the cliff without swimming if they didn't hurry. Grabbing Jennifer's hand, Randy pulled her to the edge of the sand next to the rocky cliff. He counted the waves after the big one and said, "Get ready to run after the next big wave. Five, six, seven … Now!"

They followed the wave as it slid back into the ocean, and they raced around the rocks into the next sandy wedge. "So far, so good," Randy said as he took a deep breath. "Now get ready for the next one."

"Those rocks go out farther. Maybe the tide's already too high for us to get around them. Don't let go of me," Jennifer said with her voice trembling. She held the detector tight in one hand and with the other hung onto Randy's hand as if she'd never let go.

"Ready? Here we go!" Randy shouted as the wave started back down the sandy beach. He pulled Jennifer along, swinging her around the end of the rock pile. A big wave came in before they got all the way around, and Jennifer stumbled and fell into the water, pulling Randy down with her. She tried to hold the detector up so it wouldn't get wet, but part of it did go into the water. However, the headphones were around her neck and so far had stayed above the water.

Randy struggled to get up first, pulling Jennifer up after him, and shouted, "Run before the next wave comes in!" They were able to get up to the sandy area and catch their breath. Now they had just one more cliff to get around. "I had no idea the tide would come in so quickly. We weren't in the cave very long, were we?"

"I guess we were there longer than we thought. Do you think we'll have to swim to get back to our beach?" Jennifer was worried because she didn't swim very well and was never allowed to go into the ocean without a grown-up with her.

"No, I don't think we'll have to swim. If we hurry, I think we can make it. Are you ready to run?"

"I guess so," she replied with a weak voice. "Just don't let go of me."

"I won't. Now, after the next big wave, we'll run. Ready, set … go!" Randy followed the wave out, pulling Jennifer around the rocks and up toward the beach. The next wave came in, covering their legs, but they were safe. They went a ways up from the water and flopped down in the sand all out of breath. Their hearts were pounding. "Wow! That was some trip," Randy exclaimed as he gulped for air.

"I'm not sure I want to go back to dig for the treasure." Jennifer's breathless voice was quiet and trembling. "If our parents ever found out what we did, we'd be in big trouble."

"We don't have to tell them—yet. We have to figure out a way to get back to that cave and find out what's in there." Randy was already planning the next time they would go for the treasure, assuming that what the detector registered really was a treasure. "We have to go back. I've got to know what made the static so strong and the needle move so much. I know there's something buried there, and I want to find out what it is."

WHO TO TRUST

"I'm thirsty. Let's get a soda while we decide what to do next," Jennifer said as she got up and walked over to the cooler. Randy followed. Jennifer took out the cold drinks, handed one to Randy, and sat down. She leaned against the rocky cliff and popped the soda can open. "I'm sure not going to tell anybody about what we did today. Especially our parents. Are you? They'd really be mad if they knew where we went."

Randy gulped the cold soda from the can. "Not right away, but we have to get somebody to help us the next time we go to the cave. Who do we trust?" Randy was frowning in thought. He pulled the coins out of his pocket and studied them. "We need to find out what these are and if they are worth anything. If they are, whoever we show them to will want to know where we got them. We don't dare tell, or they might go to the cave first and find our treasure before we do."

"It's our secret," Jennifer said, "and our treasure. But we do need help. Randy, I'm afraid to go back there alone. We might get caught in the cave by the tide and have to spend the night there—and with some creature! We don't know what we heard in there. I was scared. Weren't you?"

"Not really. Well … maybe a little," he admitted. "But you're right. Now who can we get to help us?" he wondered aloud. After thinking about it for a while, he finally said, "Jen, remember in school last year our teacher, Mr. Snow, talked about the time when pirates roamed the seas, stealing from ships and stashing what they stole in secret places on shore?"

"Yeah, but how can we ask him for help without telling him? What should we tell him?"

"Well, maybe he would know if pirates were ever in this area, and then he might also know how we could find out if these coins are valuable. What do you think?" Randy asked as he looked directly into Jennifer's eyes. "He'd probably not ask us a lot of questions like our parents would."

Jennifer thought about that for a while. "Good idea!" she said. "But how do we find him? School's out."

"Let's look in the phone book. Maybe we can find him listed there. Do you remember his first name?"

"I think it was something like Larry or Harry or … I'm not sure, but let's go see if we can find him."

They picked up the cooler and metal detector with the earphones and trudged through the sand to the path that led to their houses, which sat side by side high up on a cliff overlooking the beach. Both houses had a wall of windows that looked out on the expanse of the blue and green ocean.

"Let's go to my house first," Randy suggested. "Then by the time you go home, you'll be dry and won't get in trouble, which you might if your mom sees you looking like you do now. You're a mess."

"Good idea. Is your mom home?"

"Yeah, but she's always busy and won't pay that close of attention to us. It'll be okay," Randy said, feeling more relaxed about their plan.

By the time they reached the house, their clothes had dried enough so they weren't dripping. "Hi, Mom!" Randy shouted as they went in the back door. "We're back."

She answered from someplace in the house. They immediately went to the den where the phone book was. Pulling it off the shelf, Randy turned to the S's. He ran his finger down the page looking for Snow. Finding half a column of them, he said, "This may not be as simple as we first thought. There are a lot of Snows."

"Do you find a Larry or Harry Snow?"

"There's a Harold Snow. And an L. Snow and an L. J. Snow. Where shall we start?" Randy asked.

"He doesn't look like a Harold. Let's start with L. Snow. Just ask if that is the home of the teacher from school. If it isn't, say 'thanks' and hang up. Then try the next one. If we have to, we can call all the Snows in the book."

"That will take the rest of the day!"

"That's okay. We can't do anything about the treasure today anyway."

"True," Randy said as he picked up the phone and dialed the first number.

"Hello," a lady answered.

"Is this the home of Mr. Snow, the teacher at my school?" Randy asked.

"Mr. Snow does not teach at a school," she answered.

"Thank you. Sorry to have bothered you," Randy said with disappointment and hung up.

"So try the next number," Jennifer said.

He dialed that number and had the same response. By the fifth Snow, he was beginning to think his teacher was not listed. "This is the last one with an L in it. Then we'll have to think of another Snow." He dialed, and a man answered on the first ring. "Is this Mr. Snow, the teacher at my school?" Randy asked.

"I am a teacher," he said. "And who are you?"

"I'm Randy. Do you teach at the Academy?"

"Yes, I do."

"I was in your class last year. I sat right in front of your desk."

"Oh, yes, Randy. I remember you. What can I do for you?" he asked, sounding surprised and a bit curious.

"Could my friend, Jennifer, and I come over to see you? We have something we want to show you. I remember you talking about pirates and their treasures, and so we thought you might know something about what we found."

"This sounds interesting," Mr. Snow said. "Of course, I'd be glad to see you. Do you want to come over this afternoon? I'm not too busy."

"Yes, that would be great."

"Be sure to check with your parents if it's okay to come over here."

"Okay. We will. Where do you live?"

Mr. Snow gave Randy his address and directions to find the house. It was not too far from where they were, so Randy told him they would be there in a half hour.

"Jen, get your bike. We can ride over to Mr. Snow's. It's only a few blocks away. He said we could come anytime."

"Let me change my clothes first. And you'd better, too. You're a bit of a mess yourself," she said with a grin as she ran out of the room.

Jennifer entered her house through the back door and hurried to her room, hoping her mom wouldn't see her. She climbed out of her wet clothes and pulled on a dry pair of jeans and a bright blue tee shirt. She had remembered to take the shell out of her pocket. She admired it for a minute and then left it on her dresser. She slid her feet into a new pair of sandals and ran out the back door, saying, "Mom, I'll be back in about an hour."

"Jennifer, where are you going this time?" her mother asked.

"Randy and I are going for a bike ride around the neighborhood. That's all."

It was a good thing she hadn't seen Jennifer come in. She would have asked about the wet clothes. By the time Jennifer got back, her clothes would be dry, and then she'd put them in the laundry hamper. Mom would never know.

Randy was already waiting with his bicycle when Jennifer ran down the stairs. "Did you bring the coins?" she asked.

"Yeah, they're in my pocket. Come on. Let's go."

Jennifer swung her leg over the seat of her bicycle, and they rode off. They followed the directions Mr. Snow had given Randy—two blocks, then turn right to the end of the road, and then go left to the next to the last house on the right. There it was, white with light blue trim, looking just like snow. The mailbox in front had a mountain covered with snow painted on the side of it.

"This must be the right place," Randy said as he leaned his bike against the fence. "It's just as he described it."

The curtains on the window of the house next door were pulled back by an unseen hand. Jennifer knew someone was watching them before she saw the face of an old man looking out. He had a scowl on his craggy face as he kept an eye on them.

Jennifer stood her bike next to Randy's as she glanced at the window. "So let's go see what Mr. Snow has to say. I sure hope he can tell us if these are for real."

They walked up the three steps, crossed the porch to the front door, and Randy pressed the round button beside it. They heard the soft ringing of a bell. The door opened, and their teacher greeted them with a warm smile. "Come on in," he said. "It's good to see you. Have you been having a good summer?"

"Yes," Randy said, "we're having a great summer. We just celebrated our twelfth birthday and got a metal detector as a gift from our parents."

"That's quite a nice gift. Have you found anything of value yet?"

"Well, we're not sure. We went to the beach and used it today for the first time, and that's where we found what we want to show you."

"I'm eager to see what you have. You sounded a little mysterious on the phone," Mr. Snow said as he led them inside.

Randy and Jennifer walked into a large living room with windows that looked out to the ocean. There was a fireplace at one end of the room, and above it a painting of an outdoor scene with mountains covered with snow. The carpet was light blue with a white design in it. Even with the images of snow all around, the room was warm and friendly. They immediately felt relaxed as they sat side by side on the small sofa facing the windows. Mr. Snow settled into a chair beside them.

"Now, let's see what you have."

Randy pulled the coins out of his pocket but held them in his closed hand. "We can trust you to keep a secret, can't we?" he asked as he looked directly into the kind eyes of Mr. Snow.

"Of course. I promise I won't tell a soul about what you have."

Randy opened his hand to show the coins as he explained how they had found them. "They don't look like any we've seen, but we thought you might know what they are. Jennifer says they're pirates' treasure, but were pirates ever around here?"

"Yes, a long time ago pirates sailed all up and down the coast. No one has uncovered signs of their visits until recently. It was probably in the late sixteen hundreds or early seventeen hundreds that pirates freely roamed the seas in this area, taking treasure from any ship they came across. It's only been in recent years that divers have found sunken ships along the coastline. Most of them probably were sunk as a result of pirates' attacks. It was not a safe time for sailing ships. Well now, let me see what you have," he said as he reached his hand out.

Randy put the coins in his hand. "Most of these were found in a leather pouch, which was buried pretty deep in the sand and was falling apart, so we threw it away. A couple were found in other places in the sand."

Mr. Snow put his glasses on and studied the coins, turning them over and over. He moved over to the window to see them in better light. Finally he said, "These do look old and authentic. What I mean is maybe they really are very old coins from another time–even from pirates. They need to be cleaned up a bit so any imprinting on them can be read and to see if there's a date on them. If there is, that would be a good indication that they are from a time in history when pirates were here and if they are of any real value."

"How do we clean them?" Jennifer asked.

"There is an old coin dealer here in town who probably knows how to do it without damaging the coin. Let me call him," he said as he walked out of the room. In a few minutes, he came back smiling. "He says to bring them into his shop, and he will clean one for you. He has a special solution that removes the grime and stains without damaging the metal."

"Super! Where do we find him?" Randy asked.

"His shop is downtown. Do you want me to go with you?"

"Yes, that would be great. Do you have time now?" Randy asked.

"I sure do. All I was going to do was take a nap, but this is a lot more exciting. Shall we drive down in my car?"

"That would be okay, but we'd better check in with our moms first. Could we use your phone?" Jennifer asked.

"Sure. Right this way." He led them down the hall to the den where the phone was sitting on a desk covered with papers. "Excuse the mess. I was just cleaning out some files and making room for next year's school work."

Jennifer called first. "Mom, is it okay if Randy and I go downtown with Mr. Snow for a little while?" Then she had to explain who he was and, without telling her about the coins, that they were working on a project and why they wanted to go downtown. Her mom finally agreed as long as she was back in an hour.

Then Randy called his mom. She said it was all right to go since she knew Mr. Snow. But she was puzzled about what they were doing. He said he'd tell her about it later after they knew more about their project. "It's okay to go with you," he said as he hung up the phone. "We just have to be back in an hour."

Mr. Snow picked up his glasses, grabbed a jacket off the pegboard on the wall, and said, "Come on. Let's be off."

THE COIN DEALER

I t didn't take long to get downtown and find the coin shop. Mr. Snow led the way and introduced himself to the coin dealer. "I called you a few minutes ago. This is Randy and Jennifer. They have something to show you."

"Hello," the coin dealer said with a smile. "I'm Mr. George."

"Hello, Mr. George."

"So … what do you have to show me?"

Randy pulled the coins out of his pocket and placed them on the counter. "We found these at the beach and just wondered if they are of any value?"

Mr. George turned a light on and looked closely at the coins through a magnifying glass.

"They certainly are interesting," he said. "I've not seen any like this. Let's clean one up a bit and see what it might tell us." He took it into the back room. While he was gone, Jennifer and Randy looked around the shop. There were hundreds of coins and stamps in display cases. Most of them were quite old, but none looked anything like what they had found.

Mr. George returned with the coin held between a finger and his thumb. The gold sparkled in the light. "So here it is cleaned up a bit. It looks much better, doesn't it?"

"It sure does," Jennifer said. "Does it say anything? Can you read it?"

"Can you tell what it is or how old it is?" Randy asked.

"Yes, it does say something on—"

"What does it say?" Jennifer asked, interrupting him in her excitement.

"The date on it is clear, and so we know it's from the fifteenth century. It's Spanish. Where did you find this?"

Jennifer explained how they'd found the coin in a leather pouch buried in the sand at the beach. "A couple of other ones were loose in the sand."

"Well, it seems that you have found a real treasure. This would be quite valuable to a collector or a museum. Shall I clean all of them?"

Mr. Snow spoke. "I don't know if you should. If a museum were interested in them, would they want them the way the kids found them or clean?" he asked.

"That's a good question," Mr. George said as he frowned. He thought about it for a minute and then said, "Let's call a museum and find out."

He placed the call and told the director about the find and asked if he would like to see the coins. After a brief discussion, he hung up the phone and said, "The museum's curator would like to see them as they are first and then decide how to clean them. Could you take them to the museum?"

"Sure. I guess so. Where is it?" Jennifer asked.

"It's in Santa Monte, the next city down the highway." He wrote the address on a slip of paper. "Here's the address," Mr. George said as he handed it with the coin back to Randy. "Let me know what you find out."

"We will, and thanks for your help," Mr. Snow said. "Come on, kids. Let's go check this out."

"We can't do it today," Jennifer said. "We told our moms we'd be back in an hour. We've been gone at least that long already. We have to get back home."

They left the shop and jumped into the car. "Can we do it tomorrow?" Randy asked Mr. Snow. "Can you take us?"

"Sure, but what will your parents think? Maybe they'd like to take you."

"We haven't told them about our discovery yet. We thought we'd surprise them when we find out what we have," Jennifer said.

"Well, this may be quite a surprise. All right, I'll take you, but be sure your mothers know where we're going. Let them know it's an educational trip to a museum and I'm helping you with a research project. Since they both know me now, it should be okay."

A VISIT TO THE MUSEUM

Neither Randy nor Jennifer slept well that night. They were too excited about their discovered treasure and the trip to the museum the next morning. They were glad their moms didn't ask too many questions about the reason for the trip. Going with a teacher sure helped. Sometimes teachers were good to have as friends. This was one of those times. Mr. Snow had promised not to mention this to anybody. They wanted to wait until they found out what it was they had discovered, how valuable it was, and then decide what they were going to do with it.

Jennifer called Randy first thing in the morning. "Okay, Randy, what are we going to say if the museum wants our coins?" she asked.

"I'm not sure, but I don't think we can give them an answer right away. We have to find out who else might be interested and how much we can get for them. Who knows, they might try to take advantage of a couple of kids."

"You're right. We don't want to sell them to the first buyer. Let's just tell them we'll think about it."

"That's a good idea. Now get ready. I'll be over as soon as I finish my breakfast. We're being picked up at nine thirty." Randy hung up without saying good-bye.

Mr. Snow arrived right on time in front of Jennifer's house. "See you later, Mom," Jennifer said as she ran down the front steps to his car and hopped in with a cheerful, "Good morning, Mr. Snow." Randy followed close behind.

Sounding just like a teacher, he said, "Good morning, children. Did you sleep well?"

"No. I dreamed about pirates all night," Randy said.

"And I stayed awake thinking about the coins and what we should do with them. Do you think the museum will want them?" Jennifer asked.

"They might. Will you want to give them to the museum, or would you rather sell them?" Mr. Snow asked.

"If they're really valuable, I think we should sell them. We can use the money. Probably we'd have to put it in our college fund. But I guess it will depend on how much they are worth," Randy said. He was thinking about all the things he would like to buy with his share, assuming they were worth a lot.

They arrived at the museum with butterflies fluttering in their stomachs, wondering what they would find out about the coins. They entered through large glass doors and walked across the marble floor to the reception desk. Their footsteps echoed in the quiet space.

"I wonder how much the director will know," Jennifer whispered to Randy, "and how will we know if he is telling us the truth."

"We'll have to trust our teacher to tell us," Randy whispered back.

"We'd like to see the director, please," the teacher said to the receptionist. "Tell him Leonard Snow is here with some ancient artifacts."

"Wait here, please," she said with a smile at the children. She disappeared through a door behind her desk. When she came back in a few minutes, she said, "Mr. Coffman will see you in the conference room. Come this way." She led them down the hall and into a large, well-lit room. It contained a long highly polished wood table surrounded by matching chairs. "You may wait here for the director," she said as she pointed to the chairs and left the room.

In just a little while, a tall, slender man with dark hair rimming his head like a horseshoe walked into the room. "Good morning. I'm Mr. Coffman," he said as he sat down in the chair at the end of the table. "I understand you have something old to show me."

"Yes, we do. I'm Randy, and this is Jennifer," he said as he pulled the coins out of his pocket and placed them in the director's hand. "We found these at the beach yesterday."

Mr. Coffman put his glasses on his long nose. "Well, they certainly do look old," he said as he turned them over in his hand. "They need to be cleaned to really see what they are."

"We did clean one," Randy said as he showed him the one the coin dealer had cleaned.

Mr. Coffman studied it closely, noticing the date, and said, "This one looks like it is Spanish from the fifteenth century. I'd like our curator to take a look at it. Let me call him in." He used the phone sitting in the middle of the table. "Herb, I'd like you to come to the conference room and take a look at something. Can you come now? Thanks." Without taking a breath, he said, "He'll be right in, and maybe we really can find out what you have discovered."

The director asked them where they had found the coins, and while they waited for Herb, Randy and Jennifer told their story without mentioning the cave. In a few minutes, a man with snow-white hair shuffled into the room. He was wearing small rimmed glasses, which slid down nearly to the end of his nose.

"Herb, this is Jennifer and Randy, and their teacher, Leonard Snow. This is Herb Swanson. He's been with the museum since it opened, nearly forty years ago."

They each mumbled their greetings as Mr. Snow shook hands with him. Jennifer said, "I hope you can tell us what we found."

Mr. Swanson carefully sat down across from Jennifer and Randy, and Mr. Coffman handed him the coins and said, "They had this one cleaned, so we know it probably is a very old Spanish coin. But what about these others? Do you think they are from the same time?"

Mr. Swanson looked at the coins through a magnifying glass, turning them over and over. "It's hard to read, but I think they are from the same period. We'd need to clean them to be sure. Where did you find these?" he asked Jennifer. She was so excited she stumbled over her words. She told him about the metal detector and their time at the beach near their house but again didn't mention the cave.

Randy opened his mouth, closed it, took a deep breath, and asked, "Do you have any idea how valuable these would be or where they came from?

"It will take a little while to properly clean these. Then I'll do a bit of research to see what I can find out about them. Could you leave them with me and come back tomorrow? By then I should know what you have here."

"I think that would be all right," Randy said. "But—"

Mr. Snow interrupted and said, "I'm sure we can come back tomorrow. But we'd like a receipt for what we're leaving with you and the number of coins?"

"Oh, of course." Mr. Coffman picked up the phone again. "Trudy, could you come to the conference room, please? And bring your notebook. Thank you."

A plump little lady with dark hair piled up on top of her head and wearing a blue flowered dress entered the room with a notebook in one hand and a pen in the other. She smiled as she sat down in one of the chairs and adjusted her glasses as she was introduced to Jennifer, Randy, and Mr. Snow. Then Mr. Swanson and Mr. Coffman took turns telling Trudy what to write down so they could keep track of the coins the children were leaving with them. She left the room and in a few minutes returned with a typed receipt, which she handed to Mr. Coffman. He signed it, gave a copy to Randy, and he kept a copy. Randy read it carefully, showed it to both Jennifer and Mr. Show. "This looks just fine. Thanks," Randy said.

"Thank you for coming in," Mr. Coffman said as he extended his hand to Randy and then to Jennifer. Mr. Swanson slowly pushed himself up from his chair. Mr. Snow shook hands with both men, saying, "Thank you," to each of them.

As they walked out, Jennifer said, "Good-bye," over her shoulder. "See you tomorrow."

Now they had to wait another day to find out about their treasure.

THE SECRET GETS OUT

The night seemed longer than usual for both Jennifer and Randy. Jennifer kept waking up thinking about the coins and how much they might be worth. When she did sleep, strange dreams flitted through her head. Randy didn't sleep very well either. As soon as the sun came up, he rushed over to Jennifer's house. She wasn't up yet, so he threw small stones at her window. In a few minutes, her sleepy face appeared. "Come on. Get up, lazy bones," Randy said through the glass. "We have things to do."

She slid the window open. "Give me time to wake up. Come on in, and I'll be out in a minute."

Randy quietly went in the back door and waited for Jennifer. It wasn't long before she appeared looking sleepy, barefoot, but dressed.

"I hardly slept last night," she said. "I dreamed about pirates, treasure, boats, and swimming. I'm tired already. How about you?"

"Yeah, I'm kinda tired, too. Too much to think about. But it's all so exciting!"

"Let's have breakfast. Is a bowl of cereal okay?"

"Sure. That's what I usually have anyway," Randy said.

They sat at the kitchen table facing each other, lost in their own thoughts while they munched their way through the crispy flakes. "You know what I think?" Jennifer asked, and without waiting for a reply, she continued, "I think we have found real pirates' treasure and we're going to be rich and famous."

"I hope you're right," Randy said. "I guess we'll find out today when we go back to the museum."

"What did you tell your mom?"

"I didn't tell her much. I just said we didn't have enough time at the museum yesterday and we needed to go back. She said it was okay. What did your mom say?"

Jennifer was quiet for a minute and then grinned as she said, "I told her we were on a secret mission and we had to go back to the museum with Mr. Snow. She just laughed and said it sounded a bit mysterious but, as long as Mr. Snow was with us, it would be okay."

"I can only imagine what they'll say when they hear that we've discovered real treasure?"

"I have no idea, but I don't think they'll be very mad at what we've done, particularly if we get a lot of money for it."

"Let's go back to the beach before Mr. Snow comes. We have enough time. Maybe we can find some more coins," Randy said.

Jennifer carried her shoes, and Randy carried the detector. The sky and ocean were both a deep blue. The sun made the surface of the ocean look as if diamonds were scattered across blue velvet. "Oh, look, Randy," she said as she pointed to a beautiful dark pink flower. "The sand roses are in bloom."

"Yeah," he said. "But we're looking for something else today."

They walked back and forth in the sand, letting the detector just skim it, watching for a movement of the needle. They found a few bottle caps and a fifty-cent piece.

"We can use that to buy each of us a soda or something," Jennifer said. "I'd like to find more nails like the one I found yesterday. That might tell us if an old ship crashed on the rocks near here. We didn't tell Mr. Snow or the people at the museum about the nail, did we?"

"No. We can show it to them today and see what they think it's from."

They were unsuccessful in finding nails or anything else of value, and so they slowly walked back up the hill to Jennifer's house to wait for Mr. Snow. Promptly at nine thirty he drove up in front of the house.

Randy and Jennifer shouted, "Good-bye," to her mom as they ran out the door. "We'll be back some time later today!" Jennifer called over her shoulder.

After exchanging morning greetings, Mr. Snow asked, "Did you sleep well last night?"

"No," Randy answered. "I dreamed all night about pirates and treasure and stuff."

"So did I," Jennifer said. "I was so excited I could hardly get to sleep, and when I did, my dreams kept waking me up. I'll be glad when we find out what's in the—" She stopped as Randy kicked her, and then she continued, "What we have."

Randy scowled at her. She'd almost let the secret about the cave slip out. It was hard to keep it to herself.

The trip to the museum went quickly as they all talked about pirates, sailing ships, sunken vessels, and, of course, hidden treasure. But neither Randy nor Jennifer mentioned the cave and its possible treasure.

When they entered the museum, the receptionist sent them immediately to the conference room. "Mr. Coffman is expecting you."

He and Mr. Swanson both came in with smiles on their faces. "Well, Randy and Jennifer, we think you've made quite an important find," Mr. Coffman said. "Our curator researched coins of the period when these were made and has determined they are genuine gold coins from Spain."

Randy and Jennifer looked at each other, and a big grin gradually appeared on each of their faces.

"Wow!" exclaimed Randy.

"All right!" Jennifer said, giving a thumbs-up sign.

Mr. Swanson said, "Because they are solid gold, they're easy to clean. They've not been damaged from their years in the sand. They are quite valuable, but it will take a little more research to determine just how valuable. We'd love to have them in our museum."

Randy was the first to speak. "We're not sure what we want to do with them yet. We had hoped—"

Jennifer interrupted. "We'd like to think more about it once you determine their real value."

"I understand," Mr. Swanson said with a smile.

"Why don't we just wait a bit until we know what we're really working with, and we can discuss the possible purchase of them later," said the director. "Meanwhile, we'll clean the coins you left with us, and Mr. Swanson will try to discover where they may have come from and what they might be worth. Will that be all right with both of you?"

"I guess so," Jennifer said as she looked at Randy. "Since today is Thursday, why don't we check back with you Monday or Tuesday next week? That will give you time to do your research and will give us time to think about what we want to do. How does that sound?"

"Like a good plan," Mr. Coffman said as he stood up.

"One more thing," Randy said. He reached into his pocket and pulled out the square piece of metal shaped like a nail. "Do you know what this might be?"

Mr. Coffman looked closely at it and said, "Well, this seems to be a hand-made nail. People often made their own nails, say a hundred fifty to two hundred years ago in the 1800s or even earlier, and it was easier to make them in this shape than round like the ones we use today. Where did you get it?"

"We found it in the sand near where the coins were."

"I doubt that it's as old as the coins, but it could have been used in some sailing ship." Mr. Coffman frowned. "It's hard to tell where it might have come from. They were very common at one time."

"Would you like to have it for the museum?"

"Why, yes. That would be nice. We can put it with our collection of hand-made tools."

"Is that all right with you, Jennifer?" Randy asked.

She nodded and smiled. "Sure. Mr. Coffman has been a big help to us, so this is our thank you."

"Okay. It's yours," Randy said. He handed the nail to Mr. Coffman, who smiled and made a small bow as he accepted the gift.

Mr. Snow shook hands with the director. "Thanks again for your help." He turned to the children. "Come on, kids. Let's go have lunch. My treat."

"Maybe we should call our moms and tell them when to expect us home," Jennifer said.

"Good idea. I'm glad you are being so responsible. You're both getting quite grown-up." Turning to Mr. Coffman, he asked, "Could we use your phone?"

"Of course," Mr. Coffman answered. "Just dial nine to get an outside line." He and Mr. Swanson left the room.

After getting permission to have lunch with their teacher, they walked out of the museum as if in a dream. Questions were pouring out of their mouths as they drove to the restaurant. "How much money do you think we'll get?" "Who else should we show them to?" "Where can we sell them?" "What if we find more treasure in the cave?"

"What cave?" Mr. Snow asked in surprise.

"Oh dear. Now we've let it slip," Jennifer said. "Should we go ahead and tell him everything?"

"I suppose we can. He'll find out sooner or later anyway," Randy responded.

"What will I find out?" Mr. Snow asked impatiently.

They ignored Mr. Snow's questions. "Besides, we have to have someone help us if we're going back to the cave. And I'm sure we can trust Mr. Snow," Randy said as he looked into his teacher's blue eyes.

"Yes, you can trust me. Now tell me about the cave," Mr. Snow said as he parked the car.

During lunch, Randy and Jennifer took turns telling about their adventure at the beach when they used the metal detector the first time and found the small cave.

"How big is it? Are you sure it's safe to go in there?" Mr. Snow asked with his eyes wide open in surprise.

"But there's something alive in it. It scared me," Jennifer said. "I don't want to go back without a good light."

Randy continued, "The metal detector registered a find on the floor of the cave, and so we thought that's where the treasure was buried. But we need to have a shovel or a trowel or something stronger than just our fingers to dig with. The dirt and sand was packed down real hard."

"Well, I think we can handle that," Mr. Snow said. "Is it easy to get to the cave? I must admit that I'm very curious about your discovery."

"It's bit tricky, but if we did it, I'm sure you can, too. We need to find out when the tide is going to be at its lowest and then get some digging tools," Randy explained.

"Then let's go to the library on our way home and check the tide schedule," Mr. Snow said with enthusiasm.

They finished lunch quickly, and their teacher drove them to the library where he helped them find the paper with the high and low tide schedule for the week. Randy read the times for each day when the tide would be at its lowest. "According to this, Tuesday at ten o'clock in the morning should be the best time."

"That's good," Jennifer said. "We need to go to the cave when there's plenty of daylight. We want to have enough time to get back out before the tide comes in or it gets dark."

"Sounds like a plan to me," Mr. Snow said. "Do you want me to go with you Tuesday?"

"Oh, yes," Randy said. "We need help to carry the treasure back."

"I suppose you might need help, if you actually find any buried treasure," he agreed with a laugh.

"And besides," Jennifer said, "just in case there is a creature living in there, I'd feel better having a grown-up along."

"I'm not sure how much protection I'll be, but I'll do my best," Mr. Snow said with a chuckle. "Now I'd better get you two home before your mothers begin to wonder what you're up to." Mr. Snow dropped them off at Jennifer's house and waved good-bye. "See you Tuesday morning."

"I just wish we didn't have to wait so long," Randy said with impatience.

KEEPING A SECRET

The weekend was the longest Jennifer had ever known. She tried to keep busy by cleaning up her room, which normally she never did without grumbling. *I hope Mom doesn't wonder what's going on and start asking a lot of questions,* she thought. She called Randy a couple of times, but he wasn't home. *Where could he be,* she wondered. *He didn't tell me he was going away.* She was so excited and impatient, she wanted to talk to somebody—anybody. But no, she had to keep their secret. It wasn't easy to talk to her friend Allison and not tell her about their discovery.

Allison was her best friend at school, and they usually told each other everything. When she called Jennifer Saturday morning and wanted to go bike riding, Jennifer hesitated but finally said yes since Randy seemed to be gone. "Great!" Allison said. "I'll be over in a few minutes." When she arrived out of breath, they mounted their bicycles and took off down the street toward the park.

"Jen, you seem awfully quiet today. Are you okay?" Allison asked after they'd been riding for a couple of blocks.

"Yeah. I'm fine. I just have a lot of stuff going on that I'm thinking about."

"Like what?"

"Oh, just stuff," Jennifer said, trying to keep from telling her about the treasure she and Randy had found. "Like I went to the museum with Randy this week, and we saw some neat things. I've been thinking about that and how old some things are and how different they are from what we have. Just stuff like that," she said, wishing she could tell her about the gold coins.

"Going to my grandma's house is almost like going to a museum," Allison said with a laugh. "Everything in her house is old—older than her, and she's pretty old."

"Well, we saw things that were over four hundred years old. I was wondering what it would have been like living here then. Did people even live here that long ago?"

"If they did, it was probably just Indians," Allison said. "I bet they didn't live in houses, and they probably traveled on horseback or just walked."

"I wonder what kind of clothes they wore."

"You're right. It is hard to imagine what it would have been like four hundred years ago." Changing the subject, she asked, "So where have you been for the last week? I haven't heard from you."

"I'm sorry. I've just been very busy."

"I've missed you. We had a great time at your birthday party. Now that we're on vacation, I thought we could do things together. Can we go to a movie or something this week?"

"I'm not sure. I'll let you know when I have time. I'll have to check with Randy first."

They arrived at the park, left their bicycles in the rack, and walked to the swings. They settled in the seats and lazily pumped their legs to get moving. After getting as high as they could, they coasted.

"So what have you and Randy been up to?" Allison asked with a sly smile at her friend.

"We have been working on a project, and it's taking a lot of time."

"What kind of a project?"

"I'll tell you all about it later, when it's finished."

"Oh, come on. It's not like us to keep secrets from each other. You've always told me everything. You can trust me."

"I'm sure I can. It's just that I told Randy I wouldn't tell anybody until we knew what we had and—" Jennifer stopped midsentence. "And we want to … we have to … Well, we just want to get all the information together and finish the project before we share it. I'll let you know about it as soon as I can."

Allison scowled at Jennifer. "But you always tell me stuff. Why not this?"

"I just can't. Let's talk about something else."

The girls got back on their bikes and continued their chattering while they rode, but Jennifer had a hard time paying attention to what Allison was saying. Her mind kept going back to the coins, the possible treasure in the cave, how they might get it out, and what they were going to do about it.

When they got back home, Allison asked, "Jen, do you want to come to my house for lunch?"

"No, I don't think so. I've got things to do," she said. "But thanks anyway. See you later," she said as she slowly went into her house, looking up at the fragile wisps of clouds.

The first thing she did was try to call Randy again. No answer. On the third try Sunday afternoon, Randy finally answered the phone.

"Where have you been?" Jennifer asked impatiently.

"My folks took me to see my grandparents. We left early, and I didn't have time to call you. Besides, we can't do anything until Tuesday. Why? What's up?" Randy asked.

"Oh, nothing. Allison came over, and we went bike riding yesterday. I really wanted to talk to somebody. It was hard not to tell her what we are doing. I know we promised not to mention our secret to anybody."

"Did you say anything to her about, you know … what we found?"

"No, of course not. But it wasn't easy. She's my best girl friend, and I usually tell her everything. I think she knew something was up."

"Well, it won't be too long, and we can tell the whole world about it. I can hardly wait to hear what our folks will say," Randy said quietly.

Jennifer heard his mom's voice through the phone. "Say about what?"

"Oh, nothing," Randy answered her. "Just something Jen and I are doing for a summer project," he said, hoping she wouldn't ask any more questions.

"Your mom heard us?" Jennifer asked with alarm. "We better quit talking on the phone. I'll come over there. Okay?"

"Yeah, sure. See ya."

Randy met her at the back door. "That was a close one. Mom usually doesn't ask too many questions, but she wanted to know why I was being so secretive."

"What did you tell her?" Jennifer asked as they sat down on the top step.

"That Mr. Snow was helping us, and we'd show our project to her when it was finished. She seemed okay with that."

They watched the clouds turn orange, yellow, pink, and gold as the sun slid out of the sky and dipped into the ocean.

"What makes all the colors in a sunset?" Jennifer asked.

"I don't know. Maybe the sun shining through the dust or maybe the sun reflecting off the clouds. Let's ask Mr. Snow that question. He knows a lot."

"And why does the sunset have different colors from the sunrise?"

"Jen, you ask too many questions," Randy said with a laugh. Jennifer changed the subject. "I was thinking. We're going to explore the cave with Mr. Snow Tuesday, so maybe tomorrow we should call the museum to see what they have found out. I can hardly wait to hear how valuable the coins are."

"Sounds good to me," Randy said as he stood up. "I'm hungry. Let's see what we have to munch on." He led the way into his house, and they raided the fridge and cookie jar. "I hope Mom doesn't catch us. She'll tell me I'm spoiling my dinner."

"Moms always say that. We're having hamburgers tonight. You want to come over?"

"Sure, if it's okay with your mom."

"Of course. She thinks of you as part of our family anyway," Jennifer said with a big smile. "It's kind of like having a brother."

"Mom, is it okay to go to Jen's for hamburgers tonight?" he shouted.

She gave her permission, and they went next door, reminding each other not to talk about their discovery. It was hard to keep their secret during the meal.

"These sure are good hamburgers," Randy said to Jennifer's mom. "Thanks for letting me come over to eat with Jen."

"You're welcome," she said. "You two have been spending a lot of time together this week. What are you working on?" she asked.

"Oh, it's just a special project, one that we wanted to do for school. That's why we needed Mr. Snow's help," Randy answered.

"You're lucky Mr. Snow doesn't mind spending his summer vacation helping with your project. Just don't take advantage of him. He needs time off, too."

"Okay. We'll be careful," Randy answered with a glance at Jennifer.

They darted out the door as quickly as possible so there would be no more questions from Jennifer's mom.

WAİTİNG OUT THE STORM

onday morning arrived bright and sunny with none of the usual morning fog. Jennifer appeared on Randy's doorstep right after breakfast. "Randy!" she shouted. "Are you up?"

"Yeah, I'm up, but just barely. Come on in," he called from inside.

Jennifer found Randy in the den watching TV. His blond hair wasn't combed, and he didn't have his shoes on yet. "So you got up late?" she asked.

"I was kind of tired and didn't feel like getting up. How about you?"

"No problem. I'm eager to call the museum. Can we use your phone? Where's your mom? We don't want her to hear us."

Randy yawned. "I think she's in the kitchen. But it's too early to call. They aren't open yet."

"Oh, I forgot. Well, come on. Let's go down to the beach again."

Randy lazily got up from his chair, grabbed his shoes, and followed Jennifer out the door, picking up the detector on the way. Repeating their previous ventures, they searched in areas they hadn't covered before. They found a dime and a quarter.

"Not enough to make us rich," Jennifer said. "Isn't it amazing how we found the gold coins and we're not finding anything else that's valuable?"

"Just luck, I guess," Randy admitted.

After a couple of hours with nothing to show for their search, they sauntered back to the house. It was time to call the museum. Jennifer dialed the number, waited for the receptionist to put the director on the line, and took a deep breath. "Good morning, Mr. Coffman. This is Jennifer. I was wondering if Mr. Swanson had time to research the value of our gold coins?" she asked softly.

Randy held his breath, watching Jennifer's face while she waited for the director's answer.

"I understand," she said. "But we can't come on Tuesday. There's something else we have to do." She waited a little while and finally said, "So what time shall we come in Wednesday?" She hung up the phone after telling Mr. Coffman they'd be there at eleven, assuming Mr. Snow could drive them.

"So what did he say?" Randy asked, finally taking a deep breath.

"Mr. Swanson has more research to do before he can give us a definite answer. We just have to wait. But maybe that's better 'cause by then we might have found more treasure."

"That's true. Then we can negotiate a better deal," Randy said, sounding like a real businessman. "Meanwhile, let's find the tools we need to take with us to the cave tomorrow."

They gathered a trowel and a shovel, two flashlights, and a large plastic bag. "We might need something to carry the treasure in," Jennifer explained with a smile.

"Oh, sure," Randy said, "as if we'll find that much. Don't you think it's bigger than we'll need?"

"You never know," she said as she stacked everything by the back door.

"We'd better not leave all that by the door. Mom will wonder what's going on. Let's put it outside. She won't notice it there," Randy said as he picked everything up and took it out.

The sky was dark blue with a bank of clouds forming on the western horizon. A light breeze was blowing the branches of the tall pine tree, scattering needles all over the backyard.

"It would be just our luck that it'll rain tomorrow, and we won't be able to go to the cave," Jennifer said. "Do those look like rain clouds to you?" she asked, squinting at the western sky.

"I don't know. What are rain clouds supposed to look like? Are they different from regular clouds?"

"Those clouds out over the water look pretty dark to me. Little white clouds don't make rain," Jennifer said, frowning as she looked into the sky. "Tomorrow we're going into the cave to dig up our treasure. It can't rain."

"Tell that to the weather man," Randy said in jest.

During the day, the clouds got more ominous by the hour. The wind became stronger, and Randy and Jennifer found it too cold to be outside. From the upstairs window, they could see the waves splashing high against the rocks and the cliff where their treasure was hidden.

"If it's like this tomorrow, we can't go to the cave," Jennifer said with concern. "There's no way we could get around those rocks. It was hard enough to do it when the waves were just their normal size. Look at those! They're three times bigger than before."

"Yeah, I wouldn't want to be there now," Randy agreed. "Maybe by tomorrow they'll be back to normal. Let's hope so."

They sat in the den playing games, watching TV, and listening to the storm outside. It had begun to rain a couple of hours before, and it was as dark as night even though it was only mid-afternoon. They could hear the distant roll of thunder following flashes of lightning. The phone rang, and they both jumped. Randy reached for it.

"Hello. Oh, hello, Mr. Snow," he said as he looked at Jennifer. "Yes, we were thinking about tomorrow, too. Maybe it will quit raining, and we can still do what we planned." After finishing the conversation, he hung up the phone and turned to Jennifer. "He says we'll just wait until morning to see how the weather is and if the tide has gone down. We may have to postpone our adventure."

"Oh, I hope not," Jennifer moaned. "I was so excited about our project. I have such a hard time waiting. Don't you?"

"Of course, but we should go there only when we know it's safe. Don't give up on our plan. Maybe tomorrow will be a beautiful day," Randy said with more hope than he felt. The rain clouds looked as if they were here to stay. "Why don't you call your mom and ask her if you can stay for dinner? You don't want to go out in the rain now."

"You know, Randy, I'm finding it harder and harder to not tell Mom about what we're doing. I think she knows we're up to something. Every time she asks me about the project, I get butterflies in my stomach. I just say we'll tell her about it when it's finished, but I really want to tell her now. Don't you think it would be okay?"

Randy was quiet for several seconds. When he spoke, it was slow, as if he was really thinking about what to say. "Well … if you tell her … and she tells my mom, then what?"

"I'd just tell her about the coins we found—not about the cave."

"Do you think she'd keep our secret?"

"Of course, if I made her promise not to tell a soul."

"Not even my mother?"

"Absolutely. Sometimes I think maybe one of our moms should know where we go, just in case something happens and we don't get back when we're supposed to."

"Yeah, I thought about that, too. Like that time when we barely made it back from the cave and you fell down in the water. Remember?"

"Only too well."

"Wait till tomorrow to tell her. Think about it. By then we'll know if the rain is gone, and we can get back to the cave."

"Okay," Jennifer said with a sigh. Keeping secrets from her mom was not easy—even harder than keeping them from Allison.

Jennifer stayed at Randy's for dinner while huge drops of rain continued falling. The wind blew it against the windows in sheets of water.

"Well, if I'm ever going to get home, I might as well go now. Randy, may I borrow your slicker so I don't get soaked?" When she'd left her house in the morning, it was sunny. That's the way it is by the ocean. Weather can change quickly. So can plans.

All night long the storm raged. The wind howled as it swirled around the corner of the house, and the rain sounded like a dozen drummers on the window-pane. Jennifer slept fitfully, covering her head with the down pillow and trying to drown out the sounds of the storm. When she did sleep, dreams—or were they nightmares— filled her head. She was swimming hard, trying to keep her head above the waves, but as soon as she was able to catch a breath of fresh air, another wave broke over the top of her, throwing her to the sandy bottom. When she woke up in a cold sweat with her heart pounding, she threw the pillow off her head and took a deep breath. Her bedclothes were all rumpled around her as if she had been struggling to get out of them. She lay still, listening to the sounds of the waves, wind, and rain.

"Wow!" she said out loud, even though no one could hear her. "If that's what it would be like to be in the ocean during a storm, I'm never going near the water again." It was a long time before she fell into another restless sleep.

She awoke to a gray morning. The clouds had changed to a lighter color, and rain was still falling, but gently like a mist. The green numbers on her clock radio said it wasn't seven o'clock yet. *I wonder if Randy is awake, she thought. I'd like to call and see if he had nightmares last night, too.* She decided to wait a little while. She rolled out of bed feeling tired, jumped in the shower, and washed her hair. When she came in the kitchen looking for breakfast, Randy was there talking to her mom. "Hey, Randy. You're up early."

"I didn't sleep very well last night. The storm was so noisy. How about you?"

"I had nightmares all night," she said with a yawn.

"So did I," Randy said. "I dreamed we were in the ocean, and you kept going down, and I was trying to find you under big waves. You kept disappearing. It was awful. I had to come over first thing to be sure you really were still here."

"That's strange. I was dreaming the same kind of thing, only you weren't there. I was just being pushed under water by the big waves. I had a hard time breathing, but it's probably 'cause my head was under my pillow. I'm glad it was only a dream."

"Yeah, me too. Your mom said I could have breakfast with you."

"Good. I'd like the company." Jennifer smiled at him. She was glad that Randy had been trying to rescue her, even if it was only in a dream. Somehow she felt protected when he was around.

While finishing their breakfast, the sun peeked out from the clouds. "Oh, look, the sun! Maybe it will be a nice day after all!" Jennifer shouted as she jumped up and ran to the window. "Look, Randy. The sky is clearing, and there is no wind." Her mother left the kitchen, and so she continued, "The waves look much calmer than they did yesterday. Maybe we'll be able to have our outing with Mr. Snow after all. Aren't you supposed to call him this morning?"

"Yeah, he said to call around nine."

"Well, get to it then," Jennifer said. "It's already ten after."

After a brief conversation with Mr. Snow, Randy turned to Jennifer. "He said we can't be sure what the beach will look like after the storm and if the tide will be back to its normal level. We'd better check it out before we go all the way with our plan."

"Well, is he coming over?"

"Yeah, he'll be here in about half an hour."

"Let's go get our stuff from your house. Oh, dear, we left it out in the rain all night! I hope it didn't ruin anything."

They ran over to Randy's and gathered the trowel and shovel and the two flashlights, which Jennifer had thought to put in the plastic bag, and took them back to Jennifer's.

"We'd better dry everything off before it rusts," Randy said. "My dad will ground me for sure if I ruin his tools." Using an old towel, they dried everything as much as they could and then tested the flashlights and found they worked fine. "Everything's okay. We're ready to go."

"Except we haven't fixed our lunch. We'd better have one 'cause we'll probably be gone for several hours. I wonder if Mr. Snow likes peanut butter and jelly? Let's see what's in the fridge." Jennifer led the way inside and searched for something to make sandwiches. "How about ham and cheese? He should like that," she said as she pulled the packages out and put them on the counter.

Randy and Jennifer chatted easily as she made sandwiches, including peanut butter and jelly for Randy. They put them in the cooler along with sodas and some cookies and chips.

"Did you tell your mom when we'd be back?" she asked.

"I told her sometime this afternoon, probably late. She said to just be back in time for dinner. I already told her we were going to be with Mr. Snow today."

"I guess I should tell my mom the same thing. Mom," she shouted, "Randy and I will be back by dinner time! We'll be with Mr. Snow all day!"

Her answer assured them that it was okay to spend the day with him. Thank goodness their parents liked their teacher. They probably assumed the children were working on a school project. No explanation was necessary as to what they were doing or about finding treasure and searching for more. It was going to be a wonderful surprise for them—soon, they hoped.

Mr. Snow arrived just as the last of their lunch was packed into the cooler. They grabbed it, gathered up their tools, including the metal detector and headphones, and jumped into the car. They drove just out of sight of the house, parked, and then walked down to the beach. They didn't want their moms to see where they were going just yet.

"Look at the beach! It's changed from yesterday," said Randy with a puzzled look.

"The storm must have done that," Jennifer said. "There is more sand here than before. A lot got washed up on the beach. If it was like that the first time we went out with the metal detector, we'd never have found the gold coins. They would have been buried too deep."

"But this may be to our advantage now," observed Randy. "It means we can get around the end of the cliffs easier. See, the water isn't splashing as high on the rocks."

Mr. Snow had been listening to the excited conversation. Now he asked, "And just where do we go to find this treasure you think you've discovered?"

"Around the end of that cliff," Randy said as he pointed to the end of the beach. "We have to time it just right to get around without getting wet. We need to run between waves, usually after the biggest one. It's a good thing you wore your shorts 'cause long pants would get wet."

Jennifer asked, "What time is it? You said ten o'clock would be the lowest time for the tide today."

"Yes, that's what the chart in the paper said. And it's almost ten now," Mr. Snow responded.

"Maybe we should watch and count the waves between the big ones to see if they are getting lower," Randy said as if he knew how to read the ocean. "Jen, put the cooler under the rocky ledge where we did before so we can have lunch when we get back."

Jennifer walked toward the cliff looking for the space under a rocky ledge but couldn't find it. "It's not here. It disappeared. The sand must have filled it in."

"Well, just dig a hole in the sand and put it there."

Taking the shovel, she dug a space by the cliff out of the sun and put the cooler in it. "No one will ever see it here," she said as she packed the sand around it. Randy hung the headphones for the detector around his neck, and the three of them stood at the water's edge watching the waves. Jennifer carried the plastic bag containing the flashlights, and Mr. Snow had the shovel and trowel.

"We're ready for anything, now. Let's go!" Randy shouted as he led the way around the first pile of rocks.

"That was easy. The next cliff is the hardest," Jennifer told Mr. Snow. "We just have to run fast." Their feet got a little wet, but with the sand pushed up from the storm, it was easier to get around than the first time they tried it. After racing around the last bank of rocks, they reached the sandy beach in front of the cliff where the cave was. She pointed to it. "See. There it is!"

"Sure enough," Mr. Snow said with surprise. "Well, let's go see what's in there. But first, let's check our time. We want to be sure we leave before the tide comes in." He looked at his watch. "I think we have plenty of time to dig up a treasure," he said with a laugh.

THE FİRST DİG

The storm had caused the sand to pile up in front of the cave. Now they were able to climb into it with one big step. Randy entered first, followed by Jennifer and then Mr. Snow, who had to bend over to keep his head from hitting the top. They stood still for a few seconds waiting for their eyes to get used to the dark and listened for any sound that might come from the back of the cave. They heard nothing, and the flashlight showed nothing, but the cave went beyond where the light shone.

Jennifer moved to where she had felt the mound on the floor of the cave. "See, right here is where we think something is buried. Bring the detector over, Randy."

He moved it slowly over the space on the floor of the cave, and the needle did indeed move, and the static became louder. "Listen to this!" he said as he handed the headphones to Mr. Snow.

"You're right. There definitely is something down there."

"Let's start digging!" Randy said as he took the shovel. Jennifer's hands were shaking with excitement as she held the flashlight and watched him work. "This is pretty hard sand," he said as he put his foot on the shovel, pushing it into the damp sand. "I think the waves came in here last night 'cause now it's all wet."

"Do you want me to dig for a while?" Mr. Snow asked. Randy handed him the shovel and watched him as he set to work pushing it into the hard sand, lifting out a little at a time. "You're right. This is hard work," he said as he let out a puff of air. "But we'll make it. It can't be too far down."

Randy was moving from one foot to another with impatience. "I can hardly wait to see what's down there."

After several minutes, which seemed much longer to Jennifer who was still holding the light on the growing hollow, the tip of the shovel made a different sound. Mr. Snow stopped shoveling. "I think we've found something. Let's use the trowel now."

Randy dropped to his knees and began taking the sand out carefully and tossing it aside. There was a flat surface appearing with each scoop. Was it a rock or a treasure chest? It was hard to tell until more was uncovered. No one spoke. Jennifer pointed the flashlight down, and they stared into the large hole. It was at least a foot across, and Randy still had not found the edge of whatever it was they were uncovering. The pile of sand was getting bigger, and Jennifer shoved it aside to make room for more as Randy threw it out.

"Do you want me to dig for a while?" Jennifer asked.

"No, it's okay. It won't be long until we find the end of this thing, whatever it is." He tapped the trowel on the hard surface. "Listen! That doesn't sound like a rock. It sounds hollow."

"You're right! But we have only about another half hour before we should leave. The tide is starting to rise again," Mr. Snow reminded them. "Why don't you let me dig for a while?"

Randy handed the trowel to Mr. Snow. "Maybe this is just a rock. It doesn't seem to have an end to it. Perhaps if I dig some on the other side … "

"Here, let's see what the detector does." Jennifer held it over the hole. The needle jumped like crazy, and the static was so loud Randy could hear it without the headphones. "Wow! There really is something big in here!"

Mr. Snow kept digging. After a few more minutes, he had found no end to the flat surface. "I don't think it's a rock, but if it is a treasure chest, it's a very large one. We don't have time to get it out today. We'll have to leave and come back another time," Mr. Snow said with disappointment. "Perhaps tomorrow."

"Oh, we can't do that. We have an appointment at the museum tomorrow," Jennifer reminded them. "I wanted so much to have more treasure to show Mr. Coffman."

"Well, we won't be able to do that since we can't get this out, and I sure don't want to be caught here with the rising tide," Randy said as he looked out of the cave at the waves crashing on the beach.

"Maybe we could change our appointment at the museum. If they'd see us the next day, then we could come back here tomorrow. The low tide will be a little later than it was today, but we'd still have time to finish digging this thing out," Jennifer suggested.

"That's not a bad idea. What do you think, Mr. Snow?"

"I agree. It's a workable plan. Let's gather up our tools and get out of here while we can without getting too wet. You can call the museum this afternoon and change your appointment."

"We were so close! I hate to leave, but I don't want to swim out of here, so I guess we'd better go," Jennifer said. Tears of disappointment formed in her eyes.

They left the tools in the plastic bag up against the side wall of the cave and stepped out into the bright sunlight. Mr. Snow stretched as he stood upright with a groan. "Oh, that's hard on the back, staying bent over so long. You're lucky you're not too tall for that cave."

The water was rising, and it was impossible to get around the cliffs without getting wet. Randy held the detector, and Mr. Snow took hold of Jennifer's hand as they ran around the first cliff, water splashing over their feet. With Randy in the lead, hanging onto Mr. Snow's other hand, they raced around the next cliff with the receding wave.

"I'm glad we left when we did," Randy said. "Any later and we'd never have been able to run around those cliffs. We'd have had to swim."

"Well, we made it just fine," Mr. Snow said, "but I'm sure glad I had your hands to hold on to. I almost went face first in the water." They laughed at the thought of Mr. Snow sprawled in the water.

Randy dug out the cooler, and, feeling tired, they all sat down and leaned against the cliff. Jennifer pulled out the lunch she had made. "I hope you like ham and cheese sandwiches," she said to Mr. Snow as she handed him one.

"Oh, that's my favorite," he said with a smile. "I didn't expect to get lunch. This is a pleasant surprise." After a long pause, he said, "You know, this adventure makes me feel like a kid again. Thanks for including me in your secret."

"Oh, sure," Jennifer said. "We're glad you can help us, 'cause we sure need it."

They sat quietly eating, watching the sea gulls circle overhead. The waves splashing on the beach made a roar that was a backdrop to all other sounds. Randy popped open his can of soda. "What if the treasure chest is too big and heavy for us to carry out of the cave and around the cliffs? We barely made it without carrying anything."

"That would be a problem," Jennifer said, "but what a problem! Imagine having that much treasure, particularly if it's all gold."

"I think we can solve that problem when we get to it," Mr. Snow said.

"We don't even know if it is a treasure chest," Jennifer stated, "and if it is, we don't know what's in it. Randy, you worry too much."

"I'm not worrying. I just want to be prepared."

"Like a Boy Scout. Is that it?" she teased him.

"What do you think about how to get it out, Mr. Snow, especially if it's heavy?"

"Well, first let's see what we find, then we can figure out how to get it out," he said as he munched on the chips. "Say, that was a very good lunch. Thank you, Jennifer. And now, I think we'd better get going. I have things to do."

They gathered their lunch items, returning everything to the cooler, and trudged up the embankment to the car.

"Thanks for all your help today, Mr. Snow," Jennifer said. "We'll call you this afternoon to let you know what the museum says."

"Okay. I'll wait to hear from you." He dropped them off at Jennifer's house and drove off, but in the opposite direction from his house.

"I wonder where he's going?" Jennifer said, more to herself than to Randy. "You don't think he would tell our secret to anyone do you?"

"I hope not!" Randy responded. "Besides, he promised not to say anything to anyone. And teachers are supposed to keep promises."

Jennifer called the museum as soon as she got home and asked the director if he and Mr. Swanson had been able to find out about the coins and how valuable they might be. She held her breath as she waited for his answer.

"Yes," he said, "we have found that they are very rare. In fact, we've not been able to find anyone who has any like them. That makes it hard to determine their value. It may take a little longer to contact other museums and collectors to find out if any of them have coins from the same period. Would you mind if we have another day or two before meeting with you?"

"Oh, no. That would be fine. We'll call you in a couple of days." She let out a sigh of relief as she hung up the phone. "Now we can go back to the cave tomorrow," she told Randy. "They need more time. That's fine with me, because it will give us time to finish digging up the rest of our treasure."

"And then we can decide whether to offer the coins to them or maybe to contact other museums or coin dealers and figure out how much money we should get for them. I think they're worth a lot, don't you?"

"Definitely. Mr. Coffman said they couldn't find anyone else who had anything like them, so that makes them very rare. That means they're worth a lot! By the way, we promised Mr. George we'd let him know what we found out about the coins."

"Right. But not now. First, let's ride over to the library and see what we can find about pirates, treasure, gold coins, the fifteenth century, Spanish ships, and whatever," Jennifer suggested. "We have all afternoon, and I can't just sit around here waiting for tomorrow."

They rode their bikes to the library and, with the help of the librarian, found enough information to keep them reading for a couple of hours. They learned that there were lots of ships traveling along the southwest coasts in the seventeenth and eighteenth centuries.

"Listen to this," Randy said as he began to read from a book. "There were even a few ships that ventured this far from other places in the world during the fifteenth and sixteenth centuries."

"That was a long time ago," Jennifer said as she pointed to a picture of a ship in a book. "It says here that along with the shipping came pirates looking for a chance to get rich by plundering the cargo on the ships. What does plundering mean?"

"I think it means to rob, to take things by force," Randy said.

"And what about this?" she said as she began to read. "There were some ships from the East Indies and China bringing silk, rugs, jewels, and various metals. Most of the gold came from Spain."

After reading about life a couple of hundred years ago and more, they realized their life now was quite trouble free.

"I'm sure glad we didn't live here then," Jennifer said. "It would have been dangerous to live on this coast."

"Yeah, but it would have been a lot more exciting."

"Well, I don't need that kind of excitement. Come on. Let's go. I've read enough."

They put the books back on the shelf, thanked the librarian for her help, and slowly walked out the big glass doors into the bright sunlight. "Tomorrow is a long time from now," Jennifer said.

She and Randy kept busy going bike riding, playing games, watching TV, listening to music, and talking. But the thought of the treasure was never out of their minds.

A BİG PROBLEM

The next morning burst forth with bright sunlight and clear skies—a perfect day for going to the cave. They called Mr. Snow right after breakfast and made arrangements to meet him as before. They retraced their way to the beach, burying the cooler with their lunch in the same crevice by the cliff. As before, they counted the waves, and after the big one, they were able to run around the cliffs without getting too wet, and climbed up into the cave.

"Oh, look! The water came in and filled the hole we dug yesterday. How are we going to get it out so we can finish digging up the treasure?" Randy asked.

"What we need is a pail or something. We can't get it out with just a shovel," Mr. Snow said as he looked around the cave.

Randy had an idea. "I know. Let's dig a trench from the hole to the cave opening and let the water run out."

"Great idea," his teacher agreed.

Taking the trowel, Randy began digging a small channel, and Mr. Snow used the shovel to remove sand near the opening of the cave. It took quite a while because the wet sand was so firm. Finally the water began running out of the hole, and Jennifer used the trowel to help splash it out. So much time was spent removing the water that they didn't have enough time left for digging and to get the chest uncovered before they had to leave. They did find one end of it, though. "Let's dig just a little while longer and find the other end," Randy said. "I can't wait to see how big it is."

"Well, only for a few more minutes, but we can't be much longer," Mr. Snow said. Randy dug as fast as he could in the firm sand trying to find another edge. It was taking too long. "It really is about time to leave," Mr. Snow said. "We can't wait much longer."

"But what if the tide is high again tonight and water comes in? Can we build a sand wall around the hole so it won't fill with water?" Randy asked.

"Let's try it."

They all began hurrying to pile the sand around the hole, patting it down as hard as they could. They filled in the trench and built a good wall around the treasure site.

"There. That should do it, unless the tide gets too high," Mr. Snow said. They put the tools away in the plastic bag. "Now, it's time to get out of here. The tide is rising." He stood up quickly, forgetting the space was not very high. His head hit the top of the cave with a dull thud, and he slowly slumped to the floor, his head landing on the sand wall as if it were a pillow.

Randy and Jennifer stood silent, not moving, their eyes wide with shock. Mr. Snow didn't move, but he was breathing. His eyes were closed. A trickle of blood oozed from the top of his head. "Mr. Snow. Mr. Snow, are you all right?" Jennifer asked quietly. He didn't move. "Randy, what are we going to do?"

"I don't know. We have to get out … the tide is coming in." Randy's voice was a higher pitch than normal. "This is scary. What should we do?"

"We can't leave him here!" Tears of fear began forming in Jennifer's eyes.

"But we can't carry him. He's too heavy."

Jennifer thought for a minute and had an idea. "Randy, take your shirt off, and get it wet. We'll put it on Mr. Snow's head. Maybe that will bring him to."

"Good idea," he said as he slipped his tee shirt over his head. He ran to the water's edge, dipped the shirt in the water, and ran back. "Here. It's really cold."

Jennifer put the wet shirt over the top of the bleeding head and let part of it rest on his forehead. They waited, hoping it would wake him up. There was no response. The cold water did nothing. Minutes passed, and the tide was rising.

"We have to get out of here," Randy said again. "It's time to go, or we're going to get very wet. Maybe not even be able to get around the cliffs." Randy was sure they were going to be in real trouble if they had to swim around the cliffs with their teacher. They could hardly do it on their own. And then he thought about their parents. "We might have to spend the night in here. We didn't tell anyone where we were going. What will our folks do?"

"Don't panic. We have to think of something," Jennifer said as she put her head in her hands for a few seconds. Then she removed the shirt from Mr. Snow's head and handed it to Randy. "Here, go rinse this out and get it wet again. Maybe the cold will help." When Jennifer placed the fresh, cold shirt on his head, he groaned. "Wake up! Please … " she pleaded.

He slowly lifted one hand to his head and groaned again, a bit louder. "Ow!" he said as he touched the top of his head.

Jennifer lifted off the wet shirt and saw that the bleeding had nearly stopped. "Here, Randy, you better rinse this out again. You don't want your mom to see blood on your shirt. Wake up, Mr. Snow. We have to go!"

"Go where?" he asked in a weak voice.

"Out of this cave. The tide is coming in, and we're going to get wet. Here, let me help you get up."

He slowly sat up. Feeling dizzy, he started to lie down again.

"No! Come on. Sit up. We have to go!" Randy came back carrying his wet shirt.

Mr. Snow looked at him strangely and said, "What is wrong with your shirt? Do I know you?"

"It got wet, and, yes, you know me. I'm Randy."

"Oh. And who's your friend?"

"That's Jennifer." They gave a puzzled look to each other. "Come on. Let us help you get out of here."

The two of them, one on each side, helped Mr. Snow slowly stand partway up. They held him bent over and walked carefully to the entrance of the cave and down onto the sand. He stood all the way up and wavered as if he would fall. They held him and let him lean against the rocks until he was not so dizzy. The water was rising, and they still had to get him around the cliffs. They would have to go quickly, and even now there was no way they could make it without getting very wet.

"Come on, Jen. Let's go now."

"I don't want to go in the water," Mr. Snow said.

"We have to. We have to get home."

"All right." He hesitated and then continued. "But ... I don't know ... I don't remember ... Where are we?"

Randy looked at Jennifer in puzzlement. "What does he mean?"

"Maybe the bump on his head gave him amna ... am ... something. You know, when people lose their memory. I've heard of such a thing."

"I think it's amnesia," Randy told her. He turned to Mr. Snow. "What is your name?"

"My name is ... it's ... I ... I should know, but I don't think I do. I can't remember it," he replied.

"Your name is Leonard Snow. Do you remember it now?"

"Snow. That's a funny name," he said with a laugh. "Ow, my head hurts."

"Come on, Jennifer. Let's get going."

They urged Mr. Snow to walk with them to the water's edge. They held his hands, and Randy shouted, "Run, now!"

They splashed through the water, around the two cliffs, and had one more to go. Mr. Snow stopped and said, "I don't want to go any farther. I'll wait here until my head stops hurting."

"No, you won't. You have to come with us. We'll take care of your headache when we get home."

The water was higher now, and it would take all their strength to get though the waves without being knocked down by the strong current. When the wave receded, they ran through it until Mr. Snow lost his balance and fell. All three went down. The next wave covered them completely. Randy was the first to get up, sputtering but still holding the large hand of his teacher. Jennifer pulled on the other side and helped him get to his feet. They hurried toward the beach with a wave closing in on them. One last splash of cold water, and they were safe. They fell onto the dry sand, soaking wet, out of breath, and hearts pounding.

It was a while before Jennifer spoke. Whispering to Randy, she said, "Randy, if Mr. Snow really has amnesia, what should we do? We have to tell somebody. And besides, he may need a doctor."

"I know. But how can we tell the doctor or a nurse what happened without giving away our secret?"

"We better think about this."

"What secret do you have?" Mr. Snow asked.

"We'll tell you about it later. Right now we have to get you home. Are you able to walk to the car?"

"I think so. But I'm so tired."

"When you get home, you can rest. Get up now. We'll help you."

They each took hold of one of his arms and helped him up. Randy picked up the cooler, and they started up the beach toward the car.

"What's in the box?" Mr. Snow asked.

"It's our lunch," Jennifer told him. "Well, let's eat it then."

"Now?"

"Yes, now. I'm hungry."

They found a place in the sand where they could lean against the rocky cliff, and they shared the lunch Jennifer had made. Jennifer took out a soda and opened it before handing it to Mr. Snow. "Do you know where you live, Mr. Snow?" she asked while they ate their sandwiches.

"Of course. I live on … Let's see. The name of my street is … Why don't I know what it is?" He seemed a little upset by not knowing his address.

"That's okay. We'll take you home. We know where it is."

Turning to Jennifer, Randy whispered, "We have a problem!"

A TRİP TO THE HOSPİTAL

Randy and Jennifer helped Mr. Snow into his house and to his bedroom. They were getting colder by the minute from being wet, and so they knew they had to get him out of his wet clothes, and theirs also, before they all became ill. Jennifer told Randy to assist Mr. Snow if he needed help in changing his clothes while she looked for a bandage to cover the cut on his head. After he was dressed in warm, dry clothes, Jennifer took care of his head wound, cleaning it and putting a bandage where it had been bleeding.

"We have to get home and change or we'll get pneumonia. Oh, Randy, we'll have to walk home." Jennifer was shivering, and her lips were blue. "I don't want Mr. Snow to take us. He might not find his way back. I wish we had our bikes here."

"Right." He turned to his teacher, who was sitting in the large chair looking out the window toward the ocean. "Mr. Snow, we're going home to change now, and we'll be back soon. You stay right there until we get back, please."

He yawned and said, "I think I might take a little nap. I feel awfully tired." He closed his eyes, and his head rolled to one side of the chair's headrest.

Jennifer and Randy ran down the steps and into the street, continuing to run as fast as they could all the way to their houses. By the time they reached home, their clothes were nearly dry, but they were still very cold.

"Jen, as soon as I get changed, I'll come over. We have to figure out what to do with Mr. Snow. Should I tell my mom about his accident?"

"If you do, we'll have to tell her everything. Do we want to do that yet?"

"Not really, but maybe we have no choice now."

"Let's go back to Mr. Snow's and see how he is. Maybe we can find out who his doctor is, and we can call him. We'll tell him what happened, and maybe he'll tell us what to do."

"That's a good idea. See you in a few."

After changing into dry clothes and giving Jennifer enough time to dress, Randy shouted outside Jennifer's door. "Come on! Let's go!"

Jennifer bounded out of the door. They jumped on their bikes and pedaled toward Mr. Snow's house as fast as they could. "Randy, what if Mr. Snow really is hurt bad? Could we get him to drive himself to the hospital? We could tell him how to get there."

"Let's see how he is first. We have to take this one step at a time."

They arrived at the blue and white house in record time, rang the bell, and waited … and waited. After a couple more punches on the bell, they tried the door. It was unlocked, so they went in. "Mr. Snow. Are you here?" Randy shouted. No answer. When they went into the living room, they saw him sitting in the chair just as they had left him. He seemed to be sound asleep.

"Mr. Snow. Mr. Snow, wake up," Jennifer said as she gently shook his shoulder. Mr. Snow didn't move.

"He's not dead, is he?" asked Randy.

"No. He's breathing, but he won't wake up."

"Maybe he's unconscious. What should we do if he is?"

"I think it's time to call 911," Jennifer said. "I think this is an emergency, don't you?"

"Yeah, that's a good idea. But what do we tell them?"

"The truth, of course. That he hit his head. We don't have to tell them where it happened."

"I just hope they don't ask."

Randy went into the den and dialed 911. He told them about Mr. Snow and that he was alone at home, but they would stay with him until help arrived. He gave directions to the house and returned to the living room to wait.

"Since Mr. Snow didn't remember his name or where he lived, I think we'd better find his wallet, which has his driver's license in it," Jennifer said. "He may need it at the hospital."

Randy found the wallet lying on top of the dresser in his bedroom. He put it in Mr. Snow's pocket so he'd have it in case they were not allowed to go to the hospital with him. In just a few minutes, the paramedics arrived, and Randy let them in.

"What happened?" the tall young man asked.

"Well, Mr. Snow hit his head … when he fell … I think," Jennifer said hesitantly. "We let him rest a bit, but now we can't wake him up."

After a brief examination, the paramedic said, "We'll have to take him to the hospital. Can you reach his family?"

Randy quickly responded, "I don't think he has a family. I think he lives alone. We're two of his students, and we've been working on a project with him."

"Okay. We'll take him to the hospital here in town. You see if you can find any of his relatives." The paramedics put him on a stretcher and carried him to the waiting ambulance. They slid him into the open double doors, one climbed in with him; the other closed the doors and walked around to the driver's seat. Randy and Jennifer watched as the ambulance drove away with Mr. Snow.

Unfortunately the man next door was looking out the window this time. He came out on his porch and shouted at them, "What happened to Mr. Snow? What did you do to him?"

"We did nothing. He just bumped his head, but he'll be okay," Randy answered.

"Then you'd better be on your way."

"Okay. We'll just get our stuff. Will you keep an eye on his place till he comes back?"

"Yeah. I suppose so," he answered with a scowl and went back inside.

"What are we going to do now?" Randy asked Jennifer. "We don't know anything about Mr. Snow."

Jennifer pulled her face into a frown as she thought about this new problem. Suddenly she opened her eyes wide. "I know. The principal at school will know if he has any family or relatives we should call. Let's call her."

"You always have such good ideas! Jen, you are so smart."

They went in Mr. Snow's house to use the phone. "It will be okay to use his phone, won't it?" Jennifer asked. "I really don't want to wait until we get home, and also I don't want our moms to hear us just yet. We have to make a plan to let them know what's going on."

"I'm sure it's okay to call from here."

They found the phone number for Mrs. Harris, and she answered on the first ring. Jennifer started telling her that Mr. Snow had an accident and was taken to the hospital. "We need to know if he has any family so we can call them," she said. "Can you tell us if he does and how to reach them?"

Mrs. Harris said as far as she knew he did not have any. He was not married, and he never mentioned any children. "Is he going to be all right?" she asked with concern.

"I think so. He seems to have amnesia."

"I'll be happy to go down to the school and look up his records if you feel it's necessary."

"Why don't we wait and see how he is by this afternoon. You could go down to the hospital and check on him. Then can you call us?"

"Sure. I can do that."

After writing down her phone number, they checked the back door to be sure it was locked and looked to see if all the windows were closed. "Oh, dear. I just thought. What if we lock the house up and he doesn't have his keys? He can't get back in."

Randy looked on top of the dresser where he had found Mr. Snow's wallet, and sure enough, there were the keys to the house and his car. He put them in his pocket. "Okay, let's go," he said as he switched off the light. They went out, locking the front door behind them.

As they jumped on their bikes, Mister Grumpy next door came out and said, "It's about time you were out of there. It took you long enough."

They rode home quickly while trying to decide what to do next.

"Should we tell our moms what happened?" Jennifer asked.

"I think we have to. If we want to go to the hospital to see Mr. Snow, we have to ask one of them to take us. They'll want to know why."

"But we don't have to tell them where Mr. Snow got hurt. We have to keep the treasure a secret a little while longer."

They went to Jennifer's house first.

"Mom," Jennifer said. "Mom, we need to talk to you."

"Sure. What is it? What's wrong?" her mom asked as she sat down on the kitchen chair by the table. "You look upset. What happened?"

Jennifer sat across from her, and Randy stood beside her, resting his hand on the back of Jennifer's chair. She hesitated, not knowing exactly how to tell her mom what had happened. She took a deep breath. "Mr. Snow bumped his head and was taken to the hospital by ambulance."

"Oh, dear! Does he have family?" her mother asked.

"No. He lives alone. We'd like to know if he's okay. Could you take us to the hospital to see him?"

"Well, yes, I can probably do that. But where were you when he got hurt?"

"We were working on our project, and he just stood up and hit his head. We thought he'd be okay. I put a bandage on the cut, but when we couldn't wake him up, we called 911, and the paramedics took him to the hospital." Jennifer was talking fast, hoping her mother didn't ask any more questions. She didn't want to have to tell her they were in a cave at the beach.

"You did the right thing, I'm sure. Now let's go see how he's doing."

"We need to tell Randy's mom where we're going," Jennifer said, "and then we'll be right back, ready to go."

They ran next door, and Randy told his mom the same story. "Jennifer's mom is going to take us to the hospital to see him."

"We'll be back soon," Jennifer added.

"That's fine. I hope Mr. Snow will be okay."

It had been more than a couple of hours since Mr. Snow had been injured. The children expected to find him much improved. However, when they arrived at the hospital, they were told he could not have visitors yet.

"But how is he?" Jennifer pleaded. "We have to know if he's okay."

"Are you related to him?" the nurse asked.

"No. He doesn't have any family. We're his students and were working on a project with him when he was hurt. We called 911."

"I see. Well, I'm sure he'll be fine," the nurse said, "but it's too soon to know how serious the injury is. He needs to rest for a while. The doctor is taking good care of him."

"Does he remember what happened?" Randy asked.

"No. He seems to be somewhat incoherent when he's awake. Can you tell us what happened?"

Jennifer and Randy took turns telling how he had hit his head, Jennifer bandaged it, and then how they couldn't wake him up. That's when they called 911.

"Well, you did the right thing. He is awake most of the time now, but he doesn't seem to remember anything, not even his name."

They were hoping he wouldn't wake up and tell them about the cave or the treasure.

"It's too early to know, but he seems to have amnesia," the nurse continued.

"Is that serious?" Randy asked.

"No, not really. Sometimes this happens from a hard bump on the head, but usually after a few days, when the swelling goes down, the memory returns. We expect that will happen in this case," the nurse explained.

"But what if it doesn't?" Jennifer asked anxiously.

"We'll deal with that when the time comes," the nurse said. "I've got to go now and take care of my patients. Why don't you check back with us tomorrow?"

Reluctantly Jennifer and Randy nodded and turned to leave. Jennifer stopped and asked the nurse, "Since he doesn't have family that we know of, should we check with the principal at school where he teaches and see if she's found anyone we should call?"

"Why not wait until tomorrow? We don't want to alarm anyone if he's going to be okay. We can determine then what's the best thing to do," the nurse said thoughtfully. "We'll see you tomorrow then," she said with a weak smile as she turned and walked down the hall.

"I hope he's going to be okay," Jennifer said to Randy as tears were brimming in her eyes. "What if he never gets his memory back? What will we do?"

"Jen, he's going to be okay. We just have to give him time to get over the bump he got on his head. The nurse said the swelling will go down, and then we'll know."

"Mom, have you ever known anyone with amnesia?" Jennifer asked.

"No, I can't say that I have. I've read about them though. It can last from a few hours to months."

"Let's hope it doesn't take months for Mr. Snow to get over it," Randy said. "That would mean he wouldn't be able to teach at school in the fall." He was thinking about their project and the treasure they had discovered. How were they going to get it out of the cave without Mr. Snow? He and Jennifer looked at each other with concern showing on their faces. Now all they could do was wait for another day.

VİSİTİNG MR. SNOW

Jennifer and Randy were very quiet on the way home. They were worried about their teacher as well as what to do about the treasure in the cave.

"You two are awfully quiet," Jennifer's mom said. "I know you're worried about your teacher, but he has a good doctor, and I'm sure he'll be okay."

"Oh, Mom, I hope so. We need him. We haven't finished our project."

"Jen, there's no rush," Randy said. "We'll just do what we can ourselves and wait for him to get better."

"But I'm not sure we know what to do."

"We'll figure it out or … we'll just wait for Mr. Snow."

That's all they could do—wait. They'd have to call the museum to postpone their appointment. But when would they be able to go there again? They couldn't do it without Mr. Snow.

"If we asked one of our moms to take us to the museum," Jennifer whispered, "they'd find out about the treasure—at least the gold coins. Do we want to tell them yet?"

"No, not yet. I don't want them to worry. If they knew what we've done, they might want to stop us. Especially after Mr. Snow got hurt, I know my mom would flip. No. We can do this. We just have to think!"

They were quiet the rest of the way home, each hoping to find solutions to the problems.

"I don't know what we should do," Randy said as they sat on the steps at Jennifer's house.

"Let's see how Mr. Snow is tomorrow."

They sat lost in thought for several minutes.

"Jen, you're crying. What's wrong?"

"Everything! We can't get the treasure out of the cave. Mr. Snow doesn't remember anything, and he's all alone in the hospital. We can't get to the museum. We don't know what to do. Oh, Randy, what have we gotten ourselves into?"

"Yeah, things don't look too good right now. But maybe tomorrow they'll be better. Don't cry," he said as he put his arm around her. She dropped her head on his shoulder and cried. She had never done that before.

"Randy, what would I do without you?"

They sat that way until the tears stopped flowing.

"I think I'll go in now," she said. "I'll see you in the morning. Bye, and thanks."

"For what?"

"For being my friend."

Randy smiled as he walked to his house.

Sleep was a long time coming that night. Mr. Snow was on their minds, as well as the treasure. After several hours, Jennifer finally slept—and dreamed. It was the dream that helped solve the problems, but not immediately.

As soon as Jennifer woke up, she was eager to talk to Randy, and so she called him even before breakfast. "Randy, come over as soon as you can. We need to talk. I think I have an idea of what to do!"

In just a couple of minutes, he popped in the back door. "So what's up?" he asked as he sat down at the table.

"Do you want some cereal?" she asked.

"Yeah, sure. Do you have a banana?"

"Here you are. Did you sleep at all last night?"

"Some, but not very well. Are you okay this morning? You were kind of upset last night."

Jennifer smiled and said, "I'm sorry I was such a crybaby. I don't know what hit me. Anyway, I'm okay today." She took a deep breath. "I was thinking about calling the museum. What if we tell Mr. Coffman that it may be a few days before we can come in because Mr. Snow isn't well?"

"That's a good idea. Just tell him we'll call when he's better and can bring us in."

"Then I was thinking maybe we should tell at least one of our parents about the gold coins and the possible treasure. What if Mr. Snow won't be able to help us? There's no way we can get that buried chest out by ourselves."

"Yeah, I was thinking about that, too. But let's not rush into it. We need to find out how he's doing first. A few days won't make a difference. The chest isn't going anywhere."

Jennifer finished her cereal. "I'm going to call the hospital. I want to know if he's better, if he remembers anything."

Randy followed her to the den and listened as she asked the nurse how he was. "But what does he remember?" Jennifer asked. "What did he say?" She held her breath, listening to the answer. "Thank you. We'll call back later." She hung up the phone and turned to Randy. "He asked about us and wondered if we were at the cave. The nurse didn't understand what he was talking about. Golly! What if he remembers the treasure and talks about it?"

"No one would believe him—I hope."

"Maybe they'll let us see him today, and we can find out how much he remembers."

"But how can we ask him about it if Mom drives us to the hospital? She'll hear us, and then we'll have to tell her the whole story."

"Maybe it's time to do that. First, let's see what Mr. Coffman has to say."

After making the call to the museum and postponing their appointment, Jennifer asked what time her mom could drive them in to see Mr. Snow.

"Not until visiting hours. That's early afternoon. We'll go right after lunch."

The few hours to wait were spent talking about what they might get for the gold coins and what they would do with the money. They also wondered what might be in the buried chest. It was fun to dream.

"I bet it has jewels in it—diamonds, rubies, sapphires, and emeralds," Jennifer said with a dreamy look in her eyes.

"I hope it has gold coins besides jewelry. It might even have silk and stuff like we read about. I just hope that whatever it is, it's worth lots of money."

Finally it was time to go see Mr. Snow. They arrived at the exact time visiting hours were starting. Walking into his room, they saw him sleeping.

"Oh, dear. I hope he wakes up soon. We need to talk to him," Jennifer said with disappointment.

"Why don't you just sit here for a few minutes," Mom said. "He may wake up soon. I'll go to the cafeteria and get a cup of coffee." And she turned and left the room.

Jennifer stood by the bed, looking at Mr. Snow. The bandage had been removed from his head. The injury caused by the bump on the top of the cave was healing, so you could hardly see it. "Wake up, Mr. Snow," she said softly. "We want to talk to you."

He didn't move.

"I hope he's okay," Randy said as the nurse came in.

"Oh, yes. He's doing fine," she said as she crossed to the bed. She took his wrist in her hand and looked at her watch. Then she put something to his ear.

"What's that?" Randy asked.

"That's how we take his temperature. It's normal," she said as she removed it.

Mr. Snow moved and opened his eyes.

"You have some visitors. It's time to wake up," the nurse said as she raised the bed under his head and fluffed his pillow.

"Hello," Jennifer and Randy said at the same time.

Mr. Snow looked at them as if he didn't know them.

"We came to see how you are," Jennifer said. "When can you come home?"

"Let me see now. You're ... you ... your name is Jennifer and ... your friend there ... that's ... a ... let me think. That's Randy."

"Yes, that's right. Do you remember being at the beach with us?"

"Let's see. I think it was yesterday ... or maybe the day before. I can't seem to remember very well, but, yes, we were looking for something. I remember running through the waves and getting our feet wet. What a silly thing to do."

"Yes, and we got more than our feet wet," Jennifer said with a laugh. "Do you remember what we were looking for?"

"I'm not sure. Tell me. What was it?"

"We found a cave and were digging up a treasure chest," she explained. "We had to leave before we got it out because the tide was coming in. That's when you hit your head."

"You didn't tell anybody about the cave, did you?" Randy asked.

"I don't think so. I might have. I'm not sure," Mr. Snow answered.

"Do you remember where it is?"

He thought for a while as a frown formed on his forehead. "No, I can't remember."

They both let out a sigh. At least the cave was still a secret.

"That's okay," Jennifer said. "Please don't mention this to anyone. It's still a secret. We'll take you there when you're home and able to go with us again."

Jennifer's mom returned, and Jennifer introduced her to Mr. Snow. "This is my mom, and this is my teacher," she said, pointing to each one in turn.

"I had the most interesting conversation with the nurse," her mom said. "She told me you were talking about a treasure hidden in a cave."

Jennifer let out a gasp, and Randy's mouth dropped open as he looked at Mr. Snow.

"The nurse said it's typical of patients to sometimes not know the difference between imagination and reality," she continued. "You must have a very good imagination."

They laughed, and Jennifer changed the subject. "We're waiting for you to help us with our project. When will they let you come home?"

"I don't know. Let's ask," he said as he pushed the button for the nurse.

"What was the project you were working on?"

"You know. The one at the museum."

"Oh, yes. You had those old—"

"Well, it's the research we need your help with," Jennifer interrupted. "We'll talk about it when you get home."

"What is it, Mr. Snow?" the nurse asked from the doorway.

"We want to know when I can go home."

"You'll have to ask your doctor. He hasn't told me. He'll be in later."

"More waiting," said Randy. "All we do is wait."

"I think we need to let Mr. Snow rest now," Jennifer's mom said. "We can come back tomorrow."

"Oh, yes. Please do," Mr. Snow said as he closed his eyes.

"Good-bye. We'll see you tomorrow," Jennifer said.

Mr. Snow made no response. He was asleep.

WAİTING

“I’m glad Mr. Snow remembers some of the stuff we were doing. I wonder how long it will be or if he ever will remember everything.” Jennifer was walking beside Randy along the beach late in the afternoon. The sun was slipping into the ocean, leaving an array of colors in the sky.

“Do you believe in prayer, Jen?”

“Yeah, I guess. I just never thought about it much. Do you?”

“I’m not sure, but I have prayed for Mr. Snow. I didn’t know what else to do, so I figured if God hears our prayers, maybe he’d help Mr. Snow get well.”

“It sure can’t hurt, and who knows? Maybe your prayers will make a difference.”

“Look, Jen.” Randy pointed out over the ocean. “We could say God is painting a beautiful sunset.”

“Did you know that at the very instant the sun disappears into the ocean, there is a green flash of light?”

“No, I’ve never seen it.”

“Well, look for it. You can’t blink, or you’ll miss it. The sun is almost down.”

They watched in silence as the sun inched its way below the horizon, sinking into the ocean.

“I saw it! You’re right. I saw the light. Amazing!”

“Yeah, it is awesome,” Jennifer agreed.

They watched the clouds changing colors as the light slowly faded. When the first evening star appeared, Jennifer said, "Let's make a wish," and they did.

"Star light, star bright, I wish I may, I wish I might have the wish I wish tonight," Jennifer recited.

"So what did you wish for?" Randy asked.

"If you tell, it won't come true."

"Who says? I'll tell mine. I wish Mr. Snow will completely recover from the bump on his head."

"That's a good wish, and I hope it comes true, too. But I won't tell mine."

"Is a wish different from a prayer?" Randy asked as they walked back to their houses.

"Maybe it's the same thing. Mom tells me God knows what you wish for, but you don't always get your wish."

They walked in silence, each lost in their own thoughts.

"Well, g'night, Jen. See you tomorrow."

"G'night, Randy. See ya."

As Jennifer walked in the back door, her mom asked, "Where have you been? You're late for dinner."

"Oh, I'm sorry. Just walking on the beach with Randy. We saw the most awesome sunset and then wished on the evening star," she said as she sat down at the table. "Mom, do you think Mr. Snow will be okay?"

"Oh, I'm sure he will. He's improved a lot in a couple of days. Tomorrow you'll probably find out when he'll go home."

"I hope it's soon. We need his help."

"Can I help?"

"No, I don't think so. At least not yet. Maybe later. I'll let you know. If he can't take us to the museum pretty soon, could you?"

"Sure. Just let me know what day. I haven't been to the museum in a long time, and I'd enjoy a visit there."

Friday morning came with fog covering the coastline, which was typical of the summer weather. As usual, Randy came over right after breakfast.

"I wanted to go down to the beach and look for more treasure, but we don't have our metal detector. We left it in the cave when we had to help Mr. Snow out. I hope our folks don't notice we don't have it."

"They probably will assume it's at the other house. After all, we are sharing it. Let's go bike riding. I want to talk to you."

Randy looked at her with a puzzled expression. "You sound serious. Okay. Where do you want to ride?"

"Well, for one, over to Mr. Snow's place. We should check that everything is okay there. And second, not by Allison's, 'cause if she sees us, she'll want to know where we're going."

So off they went through the neighborhood, except they avoided the street where Allison lived. "That's all we need," Jennifer said, "for Allison to want to go with us. She'd have to know why we're going to Mr. Snow's house. She already wonders what you and I've been doing. I haven't talked to her for days."

The white house with blue trim looked just like always. There were newspapers on the porch, so Randy put them out of sight. "Just in case someone sees them," he said.

"What are you kids doing over there?" came a loud voice from next door.

Jennifer jumped and turned toward the sound. The old man was looking over the fence. "You shouldn't be there. What do you want?"

"We just came by to see if everything was okay here," Jennifer said in her most polite voice. "I'm Jennifer, and this is Randy."

"Well, it is, so be on your way."

A woman, who probably was the old grouch's wife, stepped out on the porch. "Who are you talking to, dear?" As soon as she saw Jennifer and Randy, she asked, "Oh, is Mr. Snow home?"

"No, just these kids are snooping around," the grouch said.

"We're not snooping," Randy said.

"Of course you're not, dear," the woman said. "Mr. Snow's been gone for a couple of days. We're wondering about him."

"He's still in the hospital," Jennifer explained. "I think he'll be home soon. We're going over to see him this afternoon. Can we give him a message?"

"Just tell him we've been keeping an eye on his place and all is well."

"It was until you two came," the old man grumbled.

"Now, dear," the woman said to her husband, "they're nice children."

"Well, we'd better be going," Jennifer said as she got on her bicycle. "And thanks for watching his place."

"Whew!" Randy exclaimed as he let out the breath he'd been holding. "You handled that really well. I thought the old man might call the cops. His wife came out just in time. She seems nice. I wonder why she married such a grouch."

"They say opposites attract."

"Is that why I like you … because you're such a grouch?" Randy teased.

"Oh, you … " Jennifer took off as fast as she could and didn't slow down until she reached her house.

"When you're mad, you sure can ride. I could hardly keep up with you."

"Jennifer, you have a message from Mr. Snow," her mom said as soon as she entered the kitchen.

"What did he say?"

"That he can come home today."

"Wonderful! But how will he get home? His car is at his house, and there's no one to pick him up." She frowned as she thought about it. "Mom, can we take him home?"

"Sure. Just give me a few … "

Jennifer was already out the door. "Randy! Randy!" she called as she ran up his back steps. "Mr. Snow is coming home!"

"Wonderful! When?"

"Today! Now! Mom said we could pick him up. Come on. Let's go. Oh … " She stopped and turned. "You'd better bring his house keys." Randy had kept them since locking up his house.

"Jen, you think of everything."

On the way to the hospital, their chatter was lively.

"I'm so glad he's coming home. Now we can work on our project again," Jennifer said with excitement.

"Remember, Mr. Snow may want to take it easy for another day or two. Don't rush him," her mom warned. "It must be quite a project. I've never seen you so excited about anything before."

"Oh, it is! I can hardly wait to show it to you, but we're not done yet."

Mr. Snow was ready and waiting to leave when Jennifer and Randy arrived at his room.

"I'm glad you're here. I'm ready to go home."

The nurse brought a wheelchair, and they pushed Mr. Snow down the corridor and out the front door into the sunlight.

"It's good to be outside again," he said as he took a deep breath of the clean fresh air and then got into the front seat of the car. Jennifer gave her mother directions to Mr. Snow's house. The old man lifted his head over the fence as the car drove in and parked. Mr. Snow got out.

"Oh, it's you," the grouchy neighbor said. "Glad you're home." And the head disappeared.

"Well, that's the nicest thing he's said to me in years," Mr. Snow said with a laugh. "He's not as bad as he sounds, though, and his wife is a dear."

Jennifer decided not to tell him about their visit the day before. Randy took the keys from his pocket and handed them to Mr. Snow. "Here, you might need these."

He let himself in and invited them all to join him.

"We'll come in just long enough to get you settled, and then we'll leave you to rest," Mom said.

Randy walked with him down the hall to his room. "Now you just lie down here on your own bed and rest. We'll come by tomorrow to see how you are. Call us if you need anything."

"All right, I will. And you're right, I am tired. I'll see you tomorrow then," he said and closed his eyes.

Now they had another day to wait.

BACK TO DİGGİNG

The following morning Jennifer awoke to bright sunlight. A perfect day to go to the beach or the museum. *I hope Mr. Snow feels good enough to go with us. I wonder if he can drive.* As soon as she finished breakfast, she got her bike, stopped to get Randy, and they went directly to Mr. Snow's. The old grouch was nowhere in sight as they went up the front steps. Mr. Snow answered the door on the first ring.

"Well, good morning. You two are out bright and early. Come on in."

"Good morning," Jennifer said with a big smile. "We wanted to be sure you're okay."

"Yes, I'm doing fine. I had a bit of a headache last night, but it's gone now. I was thinking about something you said yesterday, and I can't seem to remember everything. Can you tell me what happened? Start at the beginning."

So Jennifer and Randy told about finding the cave, uncovering what appeared to be an old chest, not getting it all uncovered, and then his head hitting the top of the cave when he stood up.

"The tide was coming in, and you were knocked out. We didn't know what to do."

"So how did you get me out?"

As they told their story, Mr. Snow was amazed at how they'd taken care of him. "I don't remember anything, except perhaps running through the water, and I thought that was just a dream.

I don't even remember going to the hospital. I owe you kids a big thank you—and more than that, it sounds like I owe you my life."

"We're just glad it all came out okay and that you are back to normal." Randy smiled. "Whatever normal is." They all laughed.

"So what do we do next?" Mr. Snow asked as he sat in his favorite chair.

"First we need to get to the museum and see what they've found out about the coins," Jennifer said. "Can you drive yet, or should we get my mom to do it? She said she would."

"Did you tell her about the coins?"

"No, just that we had more research to do. We had decided that we would tell her only if she drove us there. She'll have to find out then."

"My doctor said I shouldn't drive for a day or two, so maybe we should make an appointment for … let's see, what is today?"

"It's Saturday," Randy answered quickly. "The museum might be closed today."

"Well, why don't we plan on going Monday? That will give me the weekend to get stronger and for us to visit the cave again."

Randy's face lit up as he asked, "So when can we go to the cave? Do you really think you're up to it?"

"I think so." He stood up, wavered a little, and proceeded to the kitchen. After getting a drink of water, he came back into the room and said to Randy, "Check the tide chart for tomorrow. See if we could go sometime in the morning. I'd like to take it easy today." Mr. Snow sat down in his comfortable blue chair in front of the window overlooking the ocean.

By Sunday morning, Jennifer was eager to see Mr. Snow. When she called to see how he was, he said, "Much better. It was good to sleep in my own bed again. I think that's all I needed. So when do we go to the cave?"

"The best time is one o'clock today. Are you sure you're all right and feel like going there again?"

"Yes. I'll be fine. I'll be by for you just after noon then."

"No. We'll come over to your house this time. I don't want you driving if you don't have to. Bye."

She called Randy and told him to be ready by noon to go to the cave. "Just come over here anytime before then, and we'll ride to Mr. Snow's."

"It's a perfect day to be at the beach," Randy said when he sat in Jennifer's kitchen ready to eat a peanut butter and jelly sandwich she had made for him.

"Randy, I don't know what you'd do if they ever stopped making peanut butter. You'd probably starve to death."

"Prob'ly," he said with his mouth full.

"Do you think today will be the day we can get the chest uncovered so we can open it?"

"Unless the waves came in again and filled the hole we dug, we should be able to have it out in an hour or so."

"I hope so. I can hardly wait to see what's in it," Jennifer said with a dreamy look on her face. She sat up straight. "This is so exciting! Just think how surprised our parents will be. And when I tell Allison, she's going to be so jealous."

Randy finished the last bite of his sandwich and looked at Jennifer with a frown creasing his face. "I just had a terrible thought."

"What?"

"The chest could be empty!"

"Nobody would bury an empty chest."

"True. But what if it doesn't have anything of value in it? It could even have a skeleton or rotten food in it."

"Yuck! But you're forgetting the metal detector registered a strong signal. That means there is some kind of metal in it."

"Well, the hinges probably are metal. But you're right. I guess I'm just getting prepared for a disappointment."

"Even if there's nothing of value in it, we still have the coins we found. That's something," Jennifer said as she smiled at Randy. "It's time to go."

They shouted their good-byes and raced to their bikes. After arriving at Mr. Snow's, they followed the same routine as before and found themselves waiting for the right wave to allow them to run around the cliff. Holding hands, they dashed through the ebbing waves and then saw the hole still hiding their treasure in the cliff.

"Well, this is it," Jennifer said. "This is the day we find out what's in the chest." She took a deep breath and climbed into the cave after Randy. "Watch your head, Mr. Snow. We don't want a repeat of the other day."

"You're right. Perhaps I should have brought a hard hat," he said with a laugh. "I'll be careful."

The plastic bag with their tools was still where they'd left it. The water had not filled the hole this time. They set right to work. Jennifer held the light, Randy began removing sand from the hole, and Mr. Snow sat down and watched. After a few minutes, he said, "Here, Randy, let me do that for a while." He stood up carefully and took the shovel. Randy used the trowel to help remove sand from the hole.

"Here's the end of the chest!" shouted Randy as his trowel went deeper into the sand.

"Now that you've found the ends, all we need to do is dig out around the edges until we can open it," said Mr. Snow. "Did you find a corner?"

"No. Just an edge so far." Randy kept digging faster, following the edge and finally coming to a corner. Now they knew where to dig to get it uncovered. With Randy on one end of the hole and Mr. Snow on the other, they made good progress. They had dug so much dirt and sand out that Jennifer began pushing it out of the cave opening to make room for more.

"Do you find a handle or a lock or anything that will open this chest?" asked Mr. Snow as he sat down to rest.

"Not yet," Randy said between gasps for air. "This is hard work, but I'll make it. There has to be an end to this soon." He and Mr. Snow continued lifting sand out until they had uncovered nearly the entire top of the chest. It had taken longer than they thought, and time was running out. They had to get out of there before the tide got too high. "How much time do we have before we need to leave?"

Jennifer looked at her watch. "We really should be going soon. We've been here too long already." She looked out the opening of the cave and saw waves crashing on the small stretch of sand. "Come on. Find the latch, and then let's get out of here."

"You know," Randy said, "even if we get the entire top uncovered, we don't know how far down the latch is. It could be another foot or so if this chest is as big as I think it is."

"You're right," Mr. Snow agreed. "I think one more day of digging and we'll have our treasure. Perhaps we should come back tomorrow. I am getting a bit tired, and I don't want to have to swim out of here."

Jennifer sighed. "Oh, dear. Another day to wait. I can't stand it! I was so sure today we'd know what was in it. But you're right. We do need to get out of here."

They packed up their tools and stashed them against the wall of the cave after rebuilding the sand wall around the hole.

"There," said Randy, "we'll be back tomorrow, hopefully for the last time." He led the way out of the cave, making sure Mr. Snow kept his head down. They were getting pretty good at running around the cliffs without getting very wet.

AUTHENTIC COINS

When they arrived home, Jennifer had a message from Mr. Coffman at the museum. She called him immediately, eager to find out any news about the coins.

"Hello," she said. "This is Jennifer. What news do you have for us?" She was silent for a long time, listening.

Randy could only see her face in a frown and then a smile, her head nodding, a glance at him. "What's he saying?" he asked.

"Shh," was all she said. Then, "Thank you. That's great news! We'll call you." She hung up the phone carefully, turned to Randy, and said, "Mr. Coffman says they have determined the coins are authentic and are worth a great deal of money!" Her face broke into a grin as she jumped up and down, clapping her hands. "He said if we want to sell them, he would help us find an honest dealer, or the museum might make a decent offer for them. It's up to us. He wants us to call and let him know when we can come in."

"Wow! Does this mean we're rich?" Randy asked with a big smile spreading across his face.

"I wouldn't say that yet. But if there are more in the treasure chest, we might be. You know, we're going to have to tell our parents about the coins and the chest pretty soon. We can't make a deal with the museum or talk about selling the coins without our parents knowing."

"Yeah, I know. But let's wait until we see what's in the chest. Then we can tell them everything. We have only one more day of digging and we'll know. Then we can tell them, and the whole world!"

"You're right. One more day won't make a difference. Besides, that will give us time to talk about what we want to do with the coins. Shall we sell them? How do we know how much they're worth? Will Mr. Snow know? Do we trust Mr. Coffman and the people at the museum? We need help. Let's go over to Mr. Snow's and tell him what Mr. Coffman said about the coins. Maybe he can help us figure out what to do."

"Good idea. Come on! Let's ride!" Randy said as he jumped up out of the chair and headed for the door with Jennifer right behind him.

"Mom, we'll be back soon!" Jennifer shouted as she closed the door.

When they arrived at Mr. Snow's, they rang the bell and waited and waited and waited. They knocked and waited. No answer.

"Where could he be?" Jennifer asked. "He said he was tired and wanted to rest for a while."

"Maybe he fell asleep."

"But that was more than an hour ago. He should be awake by now." She tried the door, and it opened. "Come on. Let's go see if he's okay. Mr. Snow!" she called. "Mr. Snow, it's us. Are you okay?"

No answer. They walked through the house looking in every room and calling for their teacher. They came to his bedroom where the door was partially closed. Jennifer pushed the door open, and there he was lying on the bed, fully dressed and sound asleep.

"Should we wake him up?" Randy asked. "We made a lot of noise ringing the bell and calling to him. Maybe he's unconscious again. What if the bump on his head is still affecting him?"

"Oh dear. I hope not. Maybe he just got overtired from digging in the cave this morning."

"I think we should wake him up just to be sure he's okay," Randy said with concern. "Mr. Snow. Mr. Snow, wake up," he said rather softly. He did not stir. "Mr. Snow, please wake up," he said a little louder. He walked over to the bed and listened to his breathing. Yes, he was breathing very slowly. "Jen, what should we do?"

"I don't know, but I do think we should wake him up." She walked over by Randy and put her hand on Mr. Snow's arm. "Mr. Snow, it's Jennifer. Can you hear me? We have something to tell you."

No response.

"Randy, I think something's wrong. With all the noise we're making, he should wake up. What should we do?"

"Let's try a little harder to wake him up." He put his hand on Mr. Snow's shoulder and shook it gently. "Mr. Snow, wake up." This time he shook it harder and shouted, "Mr. Snow, wake up!"

Mr. Snow groaned and turned his head to the side, but he didn't open his eyes.

"Mr. Snow, are you okay? This is Randy. Please wake up. We have something to tell you."

Slowly Mr. Snow opened his eyes and looked at Randy standing over him. "Oh, my head hurts," he said and closed his eyes again.

"Mr. Snow, please wake up. Do you want me to get you an aspirin or something?" Jennifer asked.

"Yes, that would be nice," he mumbled. "I've got a terrible headache."

Jennifer went to the bathroom and looked in the medicine cabinet. She took two aspirin and a glass of water to Mr. Snow. "Here are the aspirin."

Randy put Mr. Snow's legs over the side of the bed and pulled him into an upright position. Mr. Snow frowned in pain and opened his eyes a little. Jennifer put the aspirin in his hand and handed him the glass of water. "Here, take these," she said.

He put the aspirin in his mouth and raised the glass to his lips. Everything he did was in slow motion. After swallowing them, he fell back on the bed and closed his eyes again.

"Poor Mr. Snow," Jennifer said. "I think he has a migraine headache. Maybe we should just let him rest today and come back tomorrow."

"You might be right. But I think we should look in on him later. Let's go for now."

"Goodbye, Mr. Snow. We'll be back later to see how you are. You just sleep some more," Randy said.

They let themselves out, making sure the door was not locked so they could get back in later. They were really concerned about Mr. Snow. Maybe he had overdone it with all the digging.

"I hope he's all right," Jennifer said. "I wish he had someone with him."

"He'll be okay until we come back. But if he's not up then, we should think about calling his doctor."

The afternoon went by slowly as they discussed what to do about the coins. "I think the museum will make a fair offer," Randy said. "It's just that we have no way of knowing the value of the coins. For instance, how much would a coin collector pay to get something like this? How much would another larger museum pay?"

"And then there is another problem we haven't thought about. If we find more coins or other valuables in the chest, do we have to let anyone else know? Since the chest is not on our property but on land that probably belongs to the state, do they have a right to it? I'm sure even Mr. Coffman would like to know where we found the coins."

"Oh, I never thought about that," Randy said with a frown creasing his forehead. "I'm sure there is no way it can be kept a secret. That's all there is to it."

"I agree. Meanwhile, what do you think we should do?" Jennifer sat with her chin in her hand as she stared at Randy.

Randy grinned at Jennifer. "You look like The Thinker sitting like that. You know, the sculpture?" Jennifer smiled. "But to answer your questions, I'm not sure right now what we should do. We need money for college, so selling the coins makes more sense than just keeping them. Let's see what Mr. Coffman offers us, and maybe the coin dealer, Mr. George, would be interested."

"That sounds like a plan," Jennifer said as she stood up. "Let's go see if Mr. Snow is awake yet. I want to be sure he is okay so we can go back to the cave tomorrow."

"And we want to tell him about the coins being authentic," Randy said.

After the short bicycle ride, they ran up the steps to Mr. Snow's front door. They rang the bell and waited. After several seconds, they were relieved to hear his call, "Come in." They found him sitting in his usual chair in the living room drinking a cup of tea.

"I'm glad you are awake. When we came by earlier, you were so sound asleep we could hardly wake you up. Do you remember us being here?" Jennifer asked.

"No. Were you here today?"

"Yes, we came by right after lunch," Randy replied. "You said you had a headache, so Jennifer gave you a couple of aspirin."

"Hmm … I don't remember that," Mr. Snow said with a puzzled look on his face. "But I'm awake now, and I feel much better."

"Good, because we wanted to tell you our exciting news," Randy said.

"And what might that be?" he asked with a smile.

Jennifer told him about the call from Mr. Coffman saying the coins were authentic and worth a great deal of money. "Now all we have to do is decide what we want to do about them. Shall we sell them to Mr. Coffman for the museum, or should we look for a buyer that might pay more? Mr. Coffman said he would help us find a buyer. Can we trust him?"

Mr. Snow was quiet for a time. "Let me think about it for a while. We need to get the chest out of the cave before we make a decision. What we find in there might make a difference on the value of the coins you already have found."

"Good thinking," Randy said. "Can we go to the cave tomorrow?"

"I think that would be a good idea. Check the paper for the low tide, and we'll go then."

Randy picked up the paper that was lying on the floor and opened it to the page listing the tides. "Low tide is a little after one tomorrow. That's a good time to go. Is that okay with you?"

"Perfect. You two be here a little after noon, and we'll go to the cave, hopefully for the last time."

"I hope so, too," Jennifer said as she twirled around. "I'm tired of waiting to find out what's in the chest."

"Tomorrow, then, will be the big day!" Randy said with excitement in his voice.

DİGGİNG OUT A CHEST

The next day dawned bright and sunny with only a few small, scattered clouds in the sky. The fog bank was far off the coast. It was a perfect day for the final digging in the cave. Jennifer woke up early with a feeling of excitement. Today was going to be a very special day. *Just think, if we found a chest full of coins, we could be millionaires. On the other hand, what if the chest doesn't have anything of value in it? All this work and waiting … worth nothing. But at least we have the few coins we did find, and they're worth something. I wonder how much,* she asked herself.

She leaped out of bed and into the shower. As soon as she was dressed, she called Randy. "Want to come over for breakfast?" she asked. "We need to talk."

"Okay," came the sleepy reply. "How come you're up so early?" he asked.

"I'm excited about today. Aren't you? This is the big day!"

"Yeah, I guess. I'm just sleepy. But okay. I'll be over as soon as I get dressed."

Jennifer went to the kitchen where her mother was drinking a cup of coffee. "Hi, Mom."

"Good morning, sweetheart," she replied. "So what are you going to do today?"

"Well, first of all, Randy is coming over for breakfast. May I make pancakes for him?"

"Sure, that'll be fine. Do you want some help?"

"No, I can do it okay. Then we're going to the beach, and we want to spend the afternoon with Mr. Snow. We think we will be finishing our project today or tomorrow."

"That's great. I'm eager to see what you've been working on."

"We are just as eager to tell you about it, too," Jennifer said with a mysterious smile forming on her lovely face.

Just then Randy popped in the back door. "Is breakfast ready yet? I'm starving."

"No, not yet. I'm making pancakes, as you can see," Jennifer said.

"Can we put chocolate chips in them? They're my favorite."

"Okay. Do you want orange juice, too? If so, you can pour it for yourself." She flipped the pancakes over and waited in silence. She was thinking about the trip to the cave. Randy drank his orange juice in one long gulp.

"They're ready," she said as she stacked them onto their plates. "They look perfect."

"Just like you," Randy said as his face turned pink. *Now what made me say that?* he wondered. But he did think Jennifer was the best friend he'd ever had, and he really enjoyed doing things with her.

"Thanks," Jennifer replied with a smile, "but I don't think that's an accurate statement. I like it all the same."

They ate their pancakes, taking bites in between their lively conversation. They talked about finishing the digging, seeing what was in the chest, getting it out of the cave and around the cliffs, and then back to the question of what to tell Mr. Coffman and their parents.

After cleaning up the kitchen, the rest of the morning was spent at the beach with their metal detector searching for anything of value. A few bottle caps and a couple of quarters were all that they uncovered. They couldn't help but think again how lucky they were to have found the old coins the first time they used the detector.

Now, today, they would find out if there was a really valuable discovery waiting for them in the buried chest.

"I think it's time to get ready to go to Mr. Snow's," Jennifer said. She was excited and wanted to be on her way to complete the digging. They'd been waiting long enough.

"But it's still early," Randy said. "Mr. Snow might not be ready yet."

"I don't care. I can't wait any longer."

"I know how you feel. This is our big day! Okay, let's go."

They arrived on their bicycles a little before noon, but Mr. Snow was already waiting for them. He even had fixed a picnic lunch for them. In the excitement of this last trip to the cave, Jennifer had forgotten all about needing a lunch.

"I'm glad you made lunch for us this time. I forgot all about it," Jennifer said.

"Well, it was my turn. You've always done it before. Now let's go see what we can find today."

They retraced their steps to the cave. The tide was low, and they were able to get around the cliffs without any problem. They found the partially dug hole just as they had left it. The hard surface of the chest was still visible. Now all they had to do was dig enough sand out so they could get to the latch and open it. Randy started the digging, and then Jennifer did some and finally gave the digging job to Mr. Snow. The sand piled up, and Jennifer pushed it out of the cave.

It wasn't long before Mr. Snow said, "I think we've got it!" He stopped digging and reached into the hole where there was a latch. It did not have a lock on it, so it could be opened easily. He pulled up, but the lid did not open. He pulled harder. No movement. "It seems to be stuck," he said. "Maybe it's rusted shut. Randy, help me pull. You pull on the lid on this side, Jennifer take the other side, and I'll pull on the latch. Now all together. One, two, three … pull!"

The lid began to lift a little. "Again. One, two, three!" They all pulled together. "It's moving! Keep pulling." Finally the lid lifted with a squeak, and they slowly opened the chest. Randy pointed the flashlight into the open space. They all looked with wide-open eyes, not knowing what they would find.

"What is it?" Jennifer asked.

"Yeah, what is that white stuff?" Randy echoed.

"Well, I don't know, but it looks like salt," Mr. Snow said. He wet the end of his finger and touched the white powdery surface. He lifted it to his tongue, let it sit in his mouth for a few seconds, and finally said, "Yes, it's salt all right."

"You mean we have found a chest full of salt? All of this waiting and work for salt? I don't believe it," Jennifer said with a touch of disappointment in her voice.

Randy asked, "Why would anyone bury a chest full of salt?"

"Well," Mr. Snow began, "hundreds of years ago salt was a valuable commodity because it wasn't readily available. In fact, in the seventeen and eighteen hundreds, there was an active black market for it, particularly in England. Probably traders in this area used it to make bargains for other things they wanted. Who knows why they, or the pirates, would bury a chest-full here. Maybe they were planning to settle in this area and could use salt to make deals with the natives. Undoubtedly, no one will ever know for sure."

"It's amazing that it has stayed good all these years," Jennifer said.

"Well, it was pretty well buried, and it stayed dry," Mr. Snow observed.

Randy asked, "Do we want to take out a chest full of salt, or shall we just leave it here? It's of no real value now since we can get all the salt we want at the market."

"I'm in favor of burying it again," Jennifer said.

"Hey! The museum might want a chest full of salt. It could be of historical interest to them."

"You're right, Randy," Mr. Snow said. "I think we should take it out."

"Whatever," Jennifer said. Tears formed in her eyes, and she plopped down on the floor of the cave and covered her face with her hands. As far as she was concerned, it really didn't matter what they did with it.

Mr. Snow lowered the lid, and he and Randy began digging a bit more around the edges so they could lift it out. It didn't take long, and they were able to get their hands under the chest. They used the shovel as leverage, and as Jennifer pushed down on the shovel, they pulled up with their hands to lift it out of the sand. Out it came with little effort. Mr. Snow took one end and Randy the other, and they struggled to carry it to the entrance of the cave. "I'll go out first," Mr. Snow said, "and then you push it out, and I'll catch it when it comes down."

Randy and Jennifer shoved the chest out the opening, and as it went down the bank, Mr. Snow caught it. As he did, he heard clinking metallic sounds. *Maybe it was just the latch,* he thought to himself. He wiggled the latch. The sound he had heard was different. It was not the latch. "Hey, kids, we need to take our tools out of the cave, too. We don't need to come back, so we had better gather everything up and take it home."

Jennifer began putting all the tools into the large garbage bag she had brought that first day. *Well, we don't need this bag for the treasure,* she thought to herself. She carried the bag of tools while Mr. Snow and Randy carried the chest between them. They were still in time to get around the cliffs without the tide being very high. It was slow moving with the heavy chest, but they made it around the first pile of rocks without a problem.

"Let's rest a minute," Mr. Snow said. "This is pretty heavy."

"Good idea. The next cliff is the worst to get around, and we don't want this chest to get wet. We'd have a solid block of wet salt," Randy said with a laugh.

After watching the waves for a while, they could tell when it was the best time to go around the rocks. That seventh wave was always the biggest, and then they got smaller. They timed it just right and were able to run around the cliff with only their feet and legs getting wet but not the chest. Only one more to get around, and they'd be able to rest again.

"What if there is someone on the beach when we come around with this chest?" Randy asked. "How do we explain this? What do we tell them?"

"Oh, I hadn't thought about that. So far we've always been the only ones here," Mr. Snow said. "I know. Jennifer, why don't you go around first, and if you see anyone, come back and let us know? If you don't see anyone, we'll bring the chest around."

"Okay," she said, feeling a little uncertain about going around alone. She set off with the bag of tools over her shoulder. After a few minutes, she returned empty handed. "All's clear!" she called.

Randy and Mr. Snow picked up the chest and trudged around the cliff. As soon as they were away from the water's edge, they set it down, letting out a puff of air at the same time.

"Whew, that was heavy," Randy said. "But I'm glad we made it."

"Now I'm hungry," Mr. Snow said. "How about lunch?" He took the container out from its hiding place and offered Randy and Jennifer sandwiches, chips, and a soda. He even remembered Randy liked peanut butter and jelly sandwiches. They were glad to rest against the cliff while munching on the delicious food. "I hope you both are not too disappointed about finding a chest full of salt. You know, it was very valuable in ancient times."

"Yes, I'm very disappointed," Jennifer said with tears forming in her eyes, "but it's only because of finding the other coins. It made us think there might be more."

"I'm just glad the coins we did find were valuable. That will be a nice surprise for our parents anyway," Randy responded.

"And you never know," Mr. Snow said, "the museum might be very interested in an old chest full of salt. I doubt if anyone has ever found one before, at least not in this state."

They finished their lunch, packed up the container, and told Jennifer to carry it to the car along with the bag full of tools. Getting the chest up the bank to the car was a challenge. It seemed to be getting heavier with every step. Just as they reached the top, Randy's hand slipped, and the chest dropped to the ground with a thud—and a clink!

"What was that?" Randy asked. "It sounded like something rattled in the chest. Salt couldn't do that."

"I thought I heard it, too, when the chest dropped out of the cave. I thought it might be the clasp. You don't suppose there is more in the chest than just salt?"

"I think we'd better take a look. But let's not do it here. Once we get it to your house, we can dig into it and see if we find anything else," Randy said.

Jennifer's excitement began to return. "Maybe they buried the treasure under the salt," she said. "Oh, I hope so! Wouldn't that be great?"

They loaded the chest into the trunk of Mr. Snow's white and blue car. Jennifer tossed the bag of tools in beside it and set the food container alongside. They climbed in the back seat as Mr. Snow started the engine. The ride to the neat little white house with blue trim didn't take very long. They quickly unloaded the trunk. As they carried the chest up the stairs, a loud voice shouted, "What've you got there?" It was the grouchy old man next door.

"Oh no," groaned Jennifer. "That's all we need. A nosy old man."

Mr. Snow replied, "Oh, just an old trunk we are going to clean up and use for storage."

"It looks kinda heavy," the old man said.

"Not really. We're just tired." What else could he say so as not to arouse his curiosity? This had to be kept a secret, at least until they found out what they had. They hurried in the front door, through the house, and out the back door, placing the chest on the enclosed back porch where it couldn't be seen from the outside.

"There. It should be okay here. Let's rest a minute. I feel like I'm getting another headache. Would you like a cup of tea?" Mr. Snow asked as he went inside.

"No thanks," Jennifer said. "I'm not that fond of tea. I'd like a soda, though, if you have one."

"So would I," Randy said quickly.

"A soda it shall be," Mr. Snow said as he reached into the refrigerator. He put the kettle on to heat water for his tea. "Let's sit a minute while the water gets hot." They all sat around his breakfast table waiting for the kettle to whistle.

"Just look at our hands!" exclaimed Jennifer as she stuck them out in front of her. "I didn't know we got so dirty."

"It was a dirty job," Mr. Snow said. "Why don't you go in and clean up a little? You know where to go."

When they came back, Mr. Snow was pouring the hot water into his cup. "Now we can relax a bit before we dig into the salt. I have no idea what we might find, but the sound we heard was metal of some kind." "I wonder what it will be?" Jennifer asked with a dreamy look that had returned to her eyes.

THE TREASURE

Mr. Snow finished his cup of tea and said, "Let's go take a look. I want to know what's in that trunk."

"So do I," Jennifer agreed as she set her empty soda can down.

Randy chimed in, "I'm sure it's real treasure!"

Mr. Snow found a large bucket and set it beside the trunk. "Okay, who wants to start removing the salt?"

"I do," Randy quickly said as he picked up the shovel.

Mr. Snow opened the lid, and Randy started lifting the salt out and putting it in the bucket. It was a lot easier than digging in the sand. Jennifer picked up the small trowel and worked at one end of the trunk to remove salt. In no time at all, the trunk was half empty. That is where they found a sheet of leather covering the entire area like a false bottom to the trunk.

"Well, whatever treasure is in here, it's under this piece of leather, which has protected it from the salt. Why don't both of you carefully lift it out and reveal the treasure?" Mr. Snow said with a smile.

Jennifer and Randy looked at each other, tentative smiles forming on their faces, and they reached into the trunk. They held the leather sheet by each corner and slowly lifted it up. Setting it to one side, three pairs of eyes looked into the hidden space. For a moment, there was only silence as no one even breathed. Then, as one, they gasped, "Wow! Look at that!"

Lying there, as they had been for a few hundred years, were more jewels than any of them had ever seen. The rainbow of color came from rubies, sapphires, emeralds, pearls, and gold. Some were mounted in pieces of jewelry; others were loose stones. And yes, among them were gold coins like those they had found in the sand, but these were in pristine condition.

"I don't believe it," said Jennifer as she stared at the treasure. "I just don't believe it!"

"It is like a dream," agreed Randy. "All this time it's been there, and just think, we are the ones to find it."

"Oh, Randy. I'm speechless," she said, grabbing him in a hug as they jumped up and down for joy.

"And we thought all we had was a box full of salt," said Mr. Snow. "Now what do we do? We can't keep this a secret."

Jennifer reached into the trunk and picked up a handful of colorful stones. She looked at each one, feeling the smooth, cool surface with her fingers. Then she picked up an emerald necklace and placed it around her neck. "I feel like a queen."

"You look like one, too, with all those jewels on you," Randy agreed, laughing. "But your clothes don't go with them."

"If these are real, this is worth a lot of money. You don't suppose there's a chance all of this is just glass, do you?" Mr. Snow asked. "Remember the story of how the Indians sold Manhattan Island for a few glass beads? If that were true, maybe that's all this is."

"We could take one or two of them to a jeweler and find out," Randy offered. "We wouldn't have to tell him where they came from."

"Good idea," said Jennifer. "Let's do it right now. Then we can figure out what we should do with all of this. There must be hundreds of stones in here."

"What should we take? An emerald, a sapphire, or a ruby?"

Mr. Snow volunteered that perhaps an emerald and a sapphire would be a good sampling. "And it might be wise to take each stone to a different jeweler so there would be fewer questions about them and we could be more sure of their authenticity. That way we could be sure of no mistake with the jeweler's opinion."

Jennifer replaced the necklace in the trunk and chose one medium-sized emerald. Randy took out a sapphire, decided it was too big and might cause suspicion, and changed it for a smaller one.

"Good choice," said Mr. Snow. "Now let's cover these up again and put the trunk in the house where we can hide it and keep the house locked. We still have time to go downtown to the jewelers today."

They left the salt out and carried the closed trunk into the house where Mr. Snow placed it in the back of his closet and covered it with some blankets. Mr. Snow looked in the phone book for a couple of local jewelers, wrote down their addresses, and said, "Let's go see what they're worth." They made sure the house was locked up tight as they left with the stones in their pockets.

Arriving at the first jewelry store, Mr. Snow said, "Let me tell them about the stone."

As they entered, the door chimed to announce their arrival. A well-dressed elderly man came from the back room. "May I help you?"

"Yes," Mr. Snow said. Handing the sapphire to him, he said, "We discovered this stone among some of my grandmother's things after she passed away, and we were wondering what it is. Is it real? Can you tell us about it?"

The jeweler looked at it carefully, took out an eyepiece, and studied it under a jeweler's lamp. He measured it in several ways, wrote down some numbers, and finally looked up at Mr. Snow. "I've not seen a stone like this in a good long time. It is a particularly fine sapphire. Do you know where it came from?"

"No, I don't. I didn't even know she had it until going through her jewelry box after her death."

"Did you want to sell it or have it set as a fine piece of jewelry?"

"I'm not sure. I was thinking of having it set as a gift for my granddaughter," he said as he glanced at Jennifer.

"It would be a very fine gift, to say the least. Do you have any idea of its value?"

"No, I was hoping you could tell me. I know nothing about gems," Mr. Snow said innocently.

"Well, my quick estimate would be that it's worth a few thousand dollars, more when it's set in a fine gold piece," the jeweler said with a smile that said he hoped he would get the job.

Wow! was all Jennifer could think. *And how many more of them are in the trunk, some of them even bigger?*

"Thank you for the information," Mr. Snow said, trying to remain casual. "We'll give some thought to a design for a setting and get back to you." He looked affectionately at Jennifer. "She's a little young right now for such a valuable gift. Could you give me a written estimate on it's value, however … for insurance purposes?"

"Of course. Just give me a few minutes."

They left the store hardly able to contain their excitement. "One more to go," said Randy. "I hope the emerald is real, too."

At the second jeweler's, Mr. Snow told the same story, handed the emerald to a well-groomed outstretched hand, and said, "We just wondered what you can tell us about this."

The jeweler's eyes opened a little wider as he turned the emerald over in his hand. "This is a beautiful stone," he said. After looking at it through a special lens and measuring it, he said, "You have a very valuable stone here. It's a good size and is as perfect as any I've seen. Did you want an estimate on it for insurance purposes?"

"Yes, that would be helpful," Mr. Snow said. "By the way, I was thinking of having it set in a piece of jewelry for my granddaughter here. Do you do that?"

"Why, of course. Would you like to look at some of our settings?" he asked as he pulled out a tray of gold and silver rings and medallions without stones. He obviously was eager to do the work.

Mr. Snow casually looked at them, asking Jennifer which ones she liked best. She couldn't make up her mind because she was in shock thinking about all the rest in the trunk back at Mr. Snow's house.

"I think we'll have to give some more thought to what we want to do," said Mr. Snow. "We will appreciate getting an estimate from you, however, and then we'll get back to you on a setting."

"Of course. Give me a moment to write it up for you."

"Boy, were you ever cool," Randy said after the jeweler left. "I almost believed your story."

"Yeah, it's kind of neat being your granddaughter," Jennifer said with a laugh.

The jeweler returned in a few minutes and handed Mr. Snow an envelope and the emerald and said, "Thanks for coming in. I enjoyed seeing and holding such a beautiful stone. I'll look forward to setting it for you ... for your granddaughter," he said as he smiled at Jennifer.

"We'll be in touch." They turned and left the store feeling as if they were walking on air. What an exciting trip this turned out to be!

In the car, Mr. Snow opened the envelope and could hardly believe his eyes. The stone was much more valuable than he would have imagined. "Kids, you are very rich, very rich indeed!"

STİLL KEEPİNG A SECRET

"I think it's time to tell your parents about your discovery, don't you?" Mr. Snow asked. "This is too big a secret to keep any longer. Also, we need to find out if it has to be reported to the State Parks Department. After all, you found it on state property."

"You're right about telling our parents," said Jennifer. "It's a secret that's hard to keep."

Randy looked concerned. "But if we report it to the state, maybe they'll keep it. It's our treasure."

"First things first. Let's find out if we have to report it or not. Again, a trip to library will give us the answer to that question." Mr. Snow certainly was a big help in knowing what to do. "Do you both have time for us to go there now?"

"What time is it?" Randy asked.

"It's just a little after three."

"Great. We have time before we have to get home. Let's hit the road again."

Mr. Snow drove them to the library, where they asked for help from the librarian in finding information of rules and regulations about the state parks. After a few minutes of reading, Randy found the section dealing with items found on state property.

"It says here that 'attempts should be made to contact the owner.' Well, that's impossible. And 'if what is found is worth more than $250,' and our find certainly is, we 'need to place an ad in the paper. If no one claims it, then the finder may take possession after ninety days, or it can be sold at auction.' Well, we know no one can claim it since whoever owned it is long since dead."

"What else does it say?" Jennifer asked.

"'If the find is worth less than $250, the finder may take possession, or it may be sold at auction.'"

"Well, we know it's definitely worth more than $250 … a lot more!" said Jennifer. "So do you think we'd have to put a notice in the paper even though we know it can't be claimed?"

Mr. Snow squinted his eyes as he thought about it. "I don't know. We may have to consult an attorney about this. It's something a bit out of the ordinary."

Randy spoke up. "Well, that part will be easy. My father is an attorney, so when we tell my parents about this, he can help us know what to do."

"Perfect! Let's go do it," Mr. Snow said.

They left the library expecting to go to Randy's house. "Oh, our bicycles are at your house. We have to get them before we go home," Jennifer remembered.

"Not only that," Randy said, "my dad won't be home until the weekend, so we can't ask him about what we have to do legally until then." Randy was thoughtful as he said, "Let's make a plan. We've been telling our parents we are working on a project with you. When our moms asked what it was, we just said we'd let them know when we're finished. Well, I think we're finished. How about this? On Saturday afternoon, you come over to my house, and all three of us will tell them about what we've discovered. We can show them some of the stones from the trunk, tell them what the jewelers said about their value, and then ask Dad if we need to report it."

"They'll probably be in a state of shock, just like we were. They may not even believe us until we show them the trunk," Jennifer said. "They'll have a lot of questions. Do we have to tell them about how we found it? You know, about going around the cliffs when it was dangerous? I don't want to get into trouble."

"We probably will have to answer their questions, but since all is well now and we have a fortune, they may not be too upset with us." Randy seemed optimistic.

"And we need to tell them about the coins. That's how we got into this in the first place," Jennifer said. "They're worth a lot, too."

"You're right. We have a lot to tell them," Randy said. "Hey, we promised to tell Mr. George what we found out about the coins. Do you think we could stop by his shop on our way home?"

"Sure, we can do that," Mr. Snow said. "I'm glad you remembered your promise."

So they stopped in and told Mr. George what the director of the museum had said about the coins. His eyes opened wide in amazement. "My, my, you certainly did make a valuable discovery. Are you interested in selling them? Even one or two? I might be interested."

"We might, but first we're waiting to find out their true value from Mr. Swanson, the museum's curator," Jennifer said. "Then we'll decide what we should do with them."

"Just remember I'm very interested," Mr. George said.

Back in the car, Mr. Snow continued talking about their plan to tell their parents. "Okay, I'll come over around three o'clock Saturday. Shall I bring the trunk?" Mr. Snow asked. "They may want to see it for themselves."

"No, let's just show them a few of the stones from it, and then maybe later they'll want to see it, and we can bring them over to your house then," Randy said. He really wanted to know how much was in the trunk before telling his parents. They hadn't taken time to really look at everything.

They arrived at Mr. Snow's where the bicycles were standing against the fence. Reluctantly they said their good-byes, knowing that on Saturday their lives would change forever.

On their way home, Randy and Jennifer talked about how they were going to tell their parents. They decided they should have Jennifer's mom go to Randy's when Mr. Snow came over so they would tell everyone at the same time. That way nothing would get left out or mixed up.

When they got home, they went to Randy's first. "Mom," Randy called, "I need to talk to you." She came into the kitchen where the two stood side by side. "Mom, will Dad be home Saturday?"

"Yes. Why?"

"You know the project Jen and I have been working on all summer? Well, it's just about finished, and we want to tell you about it when Dad's here. We have some questions he might be able to answer. Could we have Jen's mom and our teacher, Mr. Snow, come by in the afternoon, say around three o'clock?"

"I don't see why not. It sounds fine with me, but we'd better check with your dad as soon as he gets home to be sure he's not playing golf or something."

"This is so important, he will not want to play golf when we tell him about it!"

"I can hardly wait to find out what it is. It must be something really special if it would keep him from playing golf."

"Oh, it is. It is," Randy said with a big smile as they turned to leave. "We're going to Jen's to ask her mom to come over Saturday."

They left Randy's with the biggest smiles on their faces they had ever worn. They were finally going to be able to share their secret.

"Well, one thing's for sure. We've certainly learned patience in all of this," Jennifer said as they walked to her house. "Sometimes it has seemed like all we've done is wait and wait. Now we wait again until Saturday. I'll be glad when it's all over and we find out how much the treasure is worth. And you know what, Randy? We need to think about how much of the treasure belongs to Mr. Snow. 'Cause without him, we'd never have any of it."

"You're right. He deserves some of it. Do you think we should divide it equally?"

"Maybe, but I think we should have most of it since we found it. He just helped us get it out of the cave and home."

Randy thought about that for a minute. "Let's just talk to him about it. I think he'll be reasonable and fair. He may not want any of it. But let's offer it anyway."

They went in Jennifer's back door. "Mom," she called, "are you here?" No answer. "Mom, where are you? We need to talk to you."

In a few minutes, her mom entered the kitchen. "My, you've been gone a long time. Where have you been?"

"With Mr. Snow. We've just about finished our project, and we want to tell you all about it. Not right now, though. How about Saturday afternoon? Can you come over to Randy's around three o'clock, and we can tell you and his parents at the same time. Mr. Snow will be there, too."

"Sure, I can do that. This sounds very important."

"Yes, it really is. You've no idea! I can hardly wait to see your face when you see what we have."

"Then I wouldn't miss it," she said with a smile and a hug. "Now you better go get cleaned up for dinner. Randy, do you want to stay for spaghetti?"

"Sure, I'll just run and ask my mom." He was back in less than five minutes.

During dinner, Jennifer's mom asked a few questions about the project, but neither Randy nor Jennifer gave any answers that even hinted at what she was going to see.

"Mom, quit asking questions. We want it to be a surprise for you, so just wait until Saturday, please." And so they all waited.

SORTING THE TREASURE

Jennifer had wonderful dreams all night. She woke up Saturday with a smile on her face. She had been dreaming of wearing a beautiful dress and being covered in magnificent jewels. As she stretched her arms, she could imagine them with bracelets of gold, rings of sapphires and emeralds, and wondered if it was real. Did they really find a treasure chest, or did she just dream it? She bounced out of bed to look for the emerald she had shown the jeweler. There it was, tucked into her dresser drawer out of sight. It was true! They really did find treasure. And this stone was going to become a beautiful ring to remind her forever of the gift this summer's project had given her. She danced around the room holding the gleaming stone in her outstretched hand.

"Jennifer, Randy's here," her mom called. "You better get up."

Jennifer quickly hid the stone so her mom couldn't see it, not until three o'clock in the afternoon when they would tell her everything. She threw on shorts and a tee shirt, ran a brush through her long hair, and without shoes, skipped out to see Randy.

"Hey, there," she said with a big smile. "What's up?"

"Oh, nothing. I just wondered what we are going to do today," Randy said as he opened his mouth in a big yawn.

"Well, first of all, I want to eat something. Did you have breakfast already?"

"Yeah. I woke up early. I couldn't sleep. Isn't it funny how dreams can make you wake up and then you can't get back to sleep? I did lots of dreaming last night."

"Me, too. But all good stuff."

"Are we going to Mr. Snow's today to check out the project?" Randy wondered. "I'd love to see how much stuff is there."

"You're right. We never did look at everything. We need to take it all out and get to the bottom of the trunk. I'd like to know how much is there."

"So would I. Eat your breakfast, and then let's go check it out."

After finishing a big bowl of cereal and half a banana, they were ready to ride. "Mom," Jennifer shouted, "Randy and I are going bike riding! We'll be back before lunch."

When they arrived at the white and blue house, Mr. Snow was out front watering his flowers. "Well, you two are out early today," he said with a warm smile. "Are we all set for this afternoon?"

"Yes," Randy said. "Everyone will be at my house at three o'clock. I can hardly wait to tell them and see the looks on their faces. They will be so surprised."

"I'm sure they will be," Mr. Snow agreed. "We certainly were."

"We were wondering," Jennifer said, "if we should take a look at everything in the trunk. You know, just see how much there is. We didn't get to the bottom of it, so we really don't know what we have."

"You're right. Let's do it," Mr. Snow said as he turned off the water. "Come on in."

They pulled the trunk out of the closet and opened it. Jennifer gasped. There were all the beautiful jewels, just as they first saw them.

"Let's take them out and sort them by the different kinds of stones. Here will be emeralds," Jennifer said as she placed one on Mr. Snow's bed. "Here will be the sapphires, here is a place for rubies, and the pillow will be for gold. Oh, and this chair is for pearls. So let's start sorting."

One by one the stones were placed in their designated place, and they enjoyed watching the piles grow. It took a while to get to the bottom of the trunk, but finally all of the stones and gold jewelry and coins were removed and put on the bed or the chair. The necklaces and bracelets were put on another chair, and there were several of them, too. What a fortune was sitting before them! This would more than pay for their college education.

"I wonder what happened to the people who buried the trunk in that cave?" Randy said. "They must have planned to come back for it. These jewels would have provided them with a very good living."

"They probably died when their ship sank, or they were killed by the Indians when they came ashore, or maybe they forgot where they put it," Jennifer volunteered. "Imagine forgetting where you put millions of dollars worth of jewels. I never would."

"It is curious that it's been there for so many years and no one ever found it until now. It's because of the birthday gift we received from our parents, the metal detector, that we found it. Without that, it would still be buried," Randy said. "I guess we need to thank our parents for the best gift we've ever received."

"They don't know what a good investment they made with this gift," Jennifer agreed. "So now what do we do with all of this?"

Mr. Snow wrinkled his forehead and said, "Let me see if I can find something to put these into so we don't have to sort them again." He returned shortly with some glass jars. "These will work fine, and we can see the stones through them, too."

They carefully put the stones in the jars. The biggest one held the emeralds, the next held sapphires, and the smaller ones were perfect for rubies and pearls. All of the pieces that were set with jewels went into a box, and there was a separate one for the necklaces. The last jar held the gold coins like the ones they had found first. Just the coins alone were worth a fortune.

"There. All in order," Jennifer said with a sigh. "Just wait until our parents see this! They won't believe it. I can hardly believe it. If we hadn't taken those stones to the jeweler, I wouldn't."

"We really don't need the old trunk anymore. What shall we do with it?" Randy asked.

"There may be some historical value to it. I'll just hang onto it for a while. We'll be back at the museum again," Mr. Snow said, "and we can ask them if they'd be interested in it." He was thinking that it might be wise to donate some of the jewels and gold to the museum, but he'd wait to say anything until after talking with the children's parents.

"Do you want to bring these over in your car this afternoon?" Jennifer asked. "I'd love to have my parents see all of this."

"Yes, I could do that," Mr. Snow agreed. "I think I'll put them back in the trunk. I don't want the neighbors seeing me with jars full of jewels."

"Good idea," Jennifer agreed. "Can we help you?"

As they placed the jars in the trunk, Randy asked, "By the way, how is your head? Do you still have headaches?"

"No, I haven't had one for the last couple of days. I think it's all healed. That must have been quite a bump I took. I'm still amazed at how you children took care of me. Thanks again."

"No problem. I'm just glad you're okay," Randy said.

Once all of the jars and boxes were put away and placed in the trunk of Mr. Snow's car, the children headed for home.

"Wow," Jennifer said. "There were hundreds of stones. We didn't count them, but there sure were a lot."

Randy said nothing. He was lost in his own thoughts while his feet automatically kept pedaling the bike.

"Oh, look!" Jennifer said. "There's Allison. She's going to want to know what we've been doing. I haven't seen her since we got involved with our project."

"Hi, Jennifer and Randy. I haven't seen you two for ages. What have you been up to?" she asked as she rode along side of them.

"Oh, just stuff," Jennifer replied. "We just decided to go bike riding. Do you want to join us?"

"Sure. I'm not doing anything special. So how's the project?"

"Oh, ah … it's just about done," Jennifer answered hesitantly. "What have you been doing?"

"I spent some time at my grandmother's. We've been shopping for school clothes. You know, just stuff. I've missed you. I'm glad you're almost finished with that secret project so we can get together," she said with a grin, hoping they'd tell her about it.

"Yeah, me too," Jennifer said with a smile. "Maybe you can come over sometime next week, and I'll tell you all about it."

They continued chatting about nothing in particular as they rode through the neighborhood until it was time to go home for lunch … and the unveiling of the project.

UNVEILING THE PROJECT

After lunch, Jennifer helped her mom clean up the kitchen, and then she went to her room to change into fresh clothes for the visit to Randy's. Her excitement was building as she thought about what her mom would think, what she would do with all the money they would get from the found treasure, and what they should do about sharing it with Mr. Snow. She put the emerald into the pocket of her jeans and left her room ready for the unveiling of *the project.*

Randy was glad he had a little time by himself before the meeting of the families with Mr. Snow. His dad had arrived home while he was out riding with Jennifer, and his mom told him of the three o'clock visit from Mr. Snow. He was a little puzzled, and so when Randy came home, he asked him, "What's this about a project you've been working on with Mr. Snow? You're not in any trouble, are you?"

"Oh, no. It's nothing like that. But it is something quite special we think, and we wanted to share it with you and Mom and Jen's mom at the same time. And … there are a few questions … There's stuff we don't know, and we need your legal advice about what to do with it."

"This sounds important."

"Oh, it is. It's very important. You'll be amazed at what we've found … er, done."

"Okay. I'll be here at three o'clock," he said as he turned to leave the room.

After lunch, Randy spent time lying on his bed thinking about what they had discovered, how much the jewels were worth, how they were going to divide it up, and whether to sell the jewels or donate some of them to the museum. There were so many things to think about. He was glad his father was an attorney and could help them make the best and the right decisions. He dressed in clean jeans and a fresh cotton shirt.

A few minutes before three, Jennifer and her mom walked over to Randy's. This time they used the front door. After all, this was a very special visit. If only her mom knew how special. And she would in a few minutes.

Mr. Snow arrived punctually at three o'clock. He was greeted by Randy's mother at the door. "Come in, Mr. Snow. It's good to see you again." She introduced him to her husband and then Jennifer's mom.

"We met at the hospital," she said. "It's good to see you up and around. I'm glad you recovered okay."

"Me, too," Mr. Snow said with a big smile. "That was quite an experience."

As soon as everyone had said all their hellos, they were invited to sit down in the living room. "Would any of you like a glass of lemonade?" Randy's mom asked. They nodded their acceptance, and she disappeared into the kitchen. In a few minutes, she returned with a tray full of the refreshing drink and a plate of chocolate chip cookies. "Now," she said as she sat down on the sofa beside her husband, "let's hear about this project."

Jennifer, Randy, and Mr. Snow looked at each other, waiting to see who would start the story. "Go ahead. It's your project," Mr. Snow said.

Finally, Jennifer said, "It all started with the metal detector you gave Randy and me for our birthday." She and Randy took turns telling the story—how they found the coins, asking Mr. Snow about them, the visit to the museum.

"Wait a minute," Randy's father said. "The curator said they were very valuable? How valuable?"

"He didn't say just yet. They are very rare. He's found none like them. He said he should know more sometime this week," Randy answered.

"Okay. So go on."

They continued telling about the search for hidden treasure, finding the cave, Mr. Snow's bump on the head, digging up the trunk, and finding it full of salt, and then … "This." Jennifer held out her hand with the beautiful emerald in it. Randy pulled the sapphire out of his pocket and held it out beside Jennifer's hand. "And this," he said.

Their parents had sat quietly listening to the amazing story, asking questions occasionally, and now their mouths dropped open in amazement as they stared at the gems with wide open eyes. Jennifer's mom reached out to touch the stone, as if she didn't believe it was real. "How many of these were in the trunk?" she asked.

"Hundreds," Jennifer answered. "And there are rubies and pearls and gold and even some necklaces and bracelets."

"And don't forget a bucket full of salt," Randy said with a laugh.

"We took these stones to a jeweler to find out their value," Mr. Snow said. "Here is the estimate one of them gave us for Jennifer's stone." He handed the paper to her mom. "And this is for Randy's sapphire." He handed the paper to Randy's father, who let out a whistle when he saw it.

"So based on that estimate, this find is worth hundreds of thousands of dollars, perhaps millions, in addition to the few gold coins they initially found. Unbelievable!" Randy's father exclaimed.

"Dad, our question for you is, what do we have to do about reporting this? At the library, we found information about finding anything valuable on state property and how to report it. But I don't think this applies to the current laws. We need you to find out."

Randy told him what they had read at the library. "Once we find out how much everything is worth, we need to decide how to divide it up between us and Mr. Snow. Without him, we wouldn't have any of it."

Mr. Snow looked very surprised. "Why, I don't expect anything," he said.

"We just want to be fair," Jennifer said.

"That's very generous of both of you," Randy's dad said. "But first let me find out what we have to do with this unique find. Then we need to know its true worth. It may take a couple of days to determine all the answers. Let's keep this quiet for now, just between our two families and Mr. Snow. We don't want the news media to get wind of it."

"I can't believe it. I just can't," Jennifer's mom kept saying even as she held the emerald in her hand.

"Me either." Randy's mom had not said a word as she stared at the sapphire she held. It was like she was in shock. All three of them were.

"Thanks again for the metal detector," Randy said.

Jennifer chimed in, "It was the best gift ever."

"I'd say it may be the best investment we ever made." Their parents agreed on that.

"Do you want to see all of the stones that were in the trunk?" Mr. Snow asked. "I have all of them in the car."

"Absolutely," Randy's father said. He joined Mr. Snow to go to the car. "I'll help you with it."

Randy's father carried the trunk in and set it in the middle of the floor. Mr. Snow opened the top and lifted out the jars of jewels one by one, setting them on the coffee table, and then the boxes of gold and pearls.

"They don't look real. I've never seen anything so beautiful," Jennifer's mom said. "It's just amazing that anything like this exists. I wonder how long they've been buried?"

"Probably a few hundred years," Mr. Snow said. "It's hard to tell, but I'd guess it was in the fifteen hundreds or later. The dates on the gold coins probably give us a clue."

They continued looking at the wonderful colors of stones, handling the gold pieces, and speculating on where it all came from. Even Randy's mom began talking, getting more excited as the reality sunk in that she was looking at something so old and so valuable.

"Well, I'd say this certainly is a *very special project* you two have been working on this summer," Jennifer's mom said as she sat back in her chair. "If I'd known what you were up to—going in that cave and with Mr. Snow getting hurt—I'd have been worried to death. I'm still a bit upset at you doing something so dangerous without letting any of us know, but all of this helps me forgive you," she said as she gestured toward the array of colors in front of her.

"I think we'd agree with you," Randy's mom said. "But don't ever do something so dangerous again without telling us. Promise?"

"We promise," Randy and Jennifer said together as they looked at each other and smiled.

"Shall I leave all of this with you now?" asked Mr. Snow.

"Okay, but I hate to think about it being here without security protection. The bank's not open on the weekend, or I'd take it right down and put it in a safe deposit box," Randy's father said. "I'll do that first thing Monday morning. Meanwhile, we'll keep the house locked and this hidden."

Mr. Snow left, telling Randy and Jennifer that he was glad it was almost over. At least his part was. "Thanks for including me in your project. I had a great time with you two."

After thanking Mr. Snow profusely for helping the children, the two families continued talking about the discovery and what it would mean to all of them. "At least now we won't have to worry about college costs," Randy said.

"True, assuming I find out that it is yours legally," his dad said.

Jennifer felt a sense of relief now that the secret was out and she could talk to her mom about it. But she still couldn't tell Allison. She'd have to wait until Randy's father found out what they had to do about reporting it. More waiting.

ARE WE RİCH?

Monday dawned with the landscape shrouded in fog. The ocean had disappeared in the mist, but the sound of the waves breaking on the beach could be heard clearly. Jennifer was looking out the big picture window as she saw Randy emerge from the cloud surrounding the houses. She dashed to the door, pulled it open, and said, "I thought you'd never get here. The fog is so thick I thought maybe you'd lost your way."

"Never. I could find your house with my eyes shut."

She smiled at the thought. "So when is your father coming home? I'm eager to hear what he finds out about reporting our treasure."

"He said he'd try to come home early. Since he doesn't have to be in court today, he should be home around three or four o'clock. My mom wants you and your mom to come for dinner. That way we can all talk about everything."

"That's great. Let's ask Mom." They went to the kitchen where they found her making a dessert. "Mom, Randy's mom wants us to have dinner at their house tonight. Can we?"

"Oh, that would be lovely. Tell her I'll bring dessert since I'm already making this one."

The day went by slowly as Jennifer tried to read her book, but her mind kept wandering to the treasure. At last the time came to dress and go next door. She put on her new top, which brought out the dark color of her eyes. She rarely wore a dress anymore but decided this was a special occasion. She changed into a cotton dress, pulled her ponytail back, and tied it with a matching ribbon. She met her mother ready to go out the door.

"Mom, you look great! I haven't seen that dress before."

"It's new. I thought it was appropriate to wear it for this very special occasion. I see you're dressed up a bit, too. You look lovely," she said as she gave her daughter a hug. "Let's go talk about our future."

Wine was served to the parents, and Randy and Jennifer had lemonade. Finally Randy's dad spoke. "I have very good news for you. After doing a bit of research, we have determined that we do not need to report it to the state or put a notice in the paper. It's yours!"

The two children shouted "Yippee! We're rich!"

"However, once we know the value, you will have to pay taxes on it."

"How much?" Randy asked.

"I'm not sure, but we'll find out what the percentage is. It should be no problem. We can always sell a few stones to cover the tax if necessary."

"With so many, we'd hardly miss a few," Randy said with a chuckle.

During dinner, they discussed how to divide up the treasure, including some to Mr. Snow, what should be offered to the museum, and first of all, finding out what it all was worth.

"Now I can tell Allison about this secret," Jennifer said. "She's been dying to know what I've been doing all month. In fact, we can tell the whole world!"

And that's what happened. The local media came to interview the children, took pictures of the treasure, and announced to the world this major discovery by two young people. They were rich—and famous—all because of a very special birthday gift and pure luck.